"[Miller's] writing shows depth and subtlety of characterization, and a keen descriptive eye. It is well crafted and poignant, without sending readers groping for the Kleenex box."

—Speer Morgan, *The Missouri Review*

Mary Alice Goodman taught piano and lived on Jackson Street, in a house that surely cried at night. The house, although well maintained and tidy, had begun to settle rather more heavily onto its foundation as if accepting, after no more than a short struggle, the futility of resistance to gravity and heartbreak.

—from *JACKSON STREET*

"*JACKSON STREET* is powerful in such an accurate depiction of the lives, activities, and traumas of service life, especially those tinged with the Vietnam era experience. . . . Highly recommended."

—Jere Real, *Richmond Times-Dispatch*

"Deeply affecting. . . . [A] stunning little book of sweat-stained and tear-stained short stories. . . ."

—Brewster Milton Robertson,
The Island Packet (Hilton Head, SC)

Jackson Street
and Other Soldier Stories

John A. Miller

WASHINGTON SQUARE PRESS
PUBLISHED BY POCKET BOOKS

New York   London   Toronto   Sydney   Tokyo   Singapore

"The Rifle" originally appeared in *North Dakota Quarterly;* "Guns" originally appeared in *The Missouri Review;* and "Bethune, South Carolina" originally appeared in *The William & Mary Review.*

A Washington Square Press Publication of
POCKET BOOKS, a division of Simon & Schuster Inc.
1230 Avenue of the Americas, New York, NY 10020

Copyright © 1995 by John A. Miller

Published by arrangement with the author

Miller, John A., 1946–
    Jackson Street, and other soldier stories / John A. Miller.
        p.   cm.
    ISBN 0-671-56906-6
    1. Young men—Southern States—Social life and customs—Fiction.
2.United   States—Armed Forces—Recruiting, enlistments, etc.—Fiction.
3. Southern States—Social life and customs—Fiction. 4. City and town life—
Southern States—Fiction. I. Title.
PS3563.I4132J33 1997
813´.54—dc20   96-38541
                                                                              CIP

First Washington Square Press trade paperback printing March 1997

10 9 8 7 6 5 4 3 2 1

WASHINGTON SQUARE PRESS and colophon are registered
 trademarks of Simon & Schuster Inc.

Cover design by Joseph Perez

Printed in the U.S.A.

Contents

Guns

~

When Henry Teeter first arrived in Santa Monica the only thing he wanted to do was sit on the seawall at the very end of Wilshire Boulevard and watch the sunset. At several times during his pilgrimage he thought he might never get to the West Coast, and so once there he was content merely to sit quietly for a time. After seven days of heading due west from North Carolina he had turned south at Needles on the advice of a filling station attendant, who thought that Henry's old Chevrolet might have an easier go of it approaching the Pacific coast from the southeast. From Blythe to Brawley he skirted the Chocolate Mountains and kept a weather eye on the Chevy's temperature gauge. At Salton City he stopped to ponder the prehistoric Salton Sea and encountered an Airstream encampment of ancient Germans turning nut-brown in a wasteland as far removed from the *Schwarzwald* as the dark side of the moon.

"You are a soldier, *ja?*" one of the old men asked him.

Henry smiled and nodded. "Used to be," he said.

"You are welcome to stay and have dinner with us," the old man said. In the distance the low cliffs of the Orocopia Mountains hung over the brackish water of the Salton Sea like a beetling, 'pithecine brow. The old man swept his arm in a wide arc encompassing the entire group. "We have all come here to die in the sun."

The Chevrolet was knocking badly by the time Henry wound his way through Palm Springs and Riverside and on into Los Angeles proper. In Santa Monica he parked near city hall and walked across the Coast Highway to the sea-wall. The broad sidewalk was lined with towering palms and old people sitting on benches. The women wore broad-brimmed straw hats held on with diaphanous kerchiefs, and the men wore baseball caps pulled low over their spotted foreheads. Palsied hands gripped walkers, and fearful, busy eyes watched every passerby. Henry smiled at the old woman sitting closest to where he stood.

"My daughter's a lawyer," the woman said, quite out of the blue, nodding energetically, "in Century City."

Henry rented a small, one-bedroom apartment in Santa Monica and traded the Chevrolet even up for a 1969 Triumph Bonneville motorcycle. Without consciously making a decision to do so, he let his hair and beard grow, pulling his hair back into a ponytail when it was long enough. He examined himself with wonder in the mirror every morning, his appearance extraordinary for one who had lived with a GI haircut since he'd been a boy. Although his beard was flecked with gray, his hair grew thick and sensuous, as if making up for lost time. Henry was delighted with what he saw and started each day with a laugh, so taken was he with freedom.

"Why bother to come out here?" The young doctor, an internal medicine resident from UCLA on rotation to the VA hospital, examined Henry skeptically from behind the safety of the metal clipboard he was holding. "Weren't you getting adequate treatment back in North Carolina?"

Henry smiled. "They told me I could go to any VA hospital I wanted."

"That's not what I asked," the doctor said, annoyed. "Why did you come all the way out to California? Surely your doctors must have told you the extent of your condition."

Henry nodded but did not speak.

"Well," the doctor said, suddenly flipping Henry's file shut and standing up, "don't be surprised if the care you receive here isn't quite to your liking. This area is loaded with veterans, all clamoring for attention at this facility." The doctor scribbled a prescription and handed it brusquely to Henry. "When these no longer work you'll have to be hospitalized. My advice is to return to North Carolina as quickly as you possibly can."

"Fuck you," Henry muttered quietly as soon as the young man had left the examining room.

Santa Monica was vaguely troubling to Henry, a place in which he had no particular wish to die. He couldn't quite put his finger on it but decided that it had something to do with all the old people sitting on the benches along the seawall. He had come to California for no other reason than that, in twenty-eight years in the army, he had never been there before. In countless dayrooms, squad bays, and transient barracks, he had heard men speak of it the way a soldier speaks of a woman pictured in a cigarette or liquor advertisement torn out of a magazine and hidden away in a footlocker. *California*, some kid from Cleveland, or Pittsburgh, or Toccoa, Georgia, would say, *man, what I wouldn't give to be there now*. Most everyone listening would nod silently, the sentiment universal.

"Wow, look at those guns," said the young woman standing next to Henry.

He had stopped to watch a bodybuilder being photographed on Venice Beach. He glanced at the woman. "Guns?"

She looked at him warily. "Yeah," she said, "guns." She mimicked the bodybuilder's pose, flexing her arms. "You know, his arms. His guns. Jeez," she rolled her eyes at one of the other bystanders, "did you just, like, land on this planet, or what?"

Henry was so taken with Venice Beach that he moved there from Santa Monica the next day. His landlady in Santa Monica hated to see him leave.

"A nice man like you," she said, watching him pack his few

belongings into an old duffel bag, "should stay here. Venice Beach is for kids. Crazies. Listen to me. Somebody will hit you on the head and take your money." She paused to shake her head, astonished at the very thought. "You don't know from Venice Beach, believe me."

"So, like, what do you do?" Bonnie asked him.

"Not much," Henry answered, nodding for more coffee. "I guess you could say that I'm out here just sort of enjoying myself."

"You mean, like, retired?"

"Yeah," Henry said, "like retired."

"You don't look old enough to be retired," Bonnie said doubtfully, still holding the coffeepot. She glanced quickly over her left shoulder to make sure that Eddie the bartender wasn't eavesdropping on their conversation. "Would you like to go out with me tonight? After I get off work?"

Henry smiled. "Don't you have a steady young man you'd rather be with?"

"Does that mean, like, you don't want to?"

"No, no," Henry said, afraid he had hurt her feelings, "it's not that. What time do you get off work?"

"At midnight."

Bonnie sat behind Henry on the Triumph and hugged him tightly. She had to hike her skirt well up on her thighs to get on the motorcycle, and she wished her friends could see her.

"Actually, I'm an actress," she told Henry after they had ordered Coronas at a bar not far down the beach from where she worked. "Being a waitress is just a sort of temporary thing for me."

Henry nodded solemnly but didn't say anything.

"My friends think I look like Meryl Streep."

Henry had no idea who Meryl Streep was. "I believe I can see a likeness there," he said.

"What kind of work are you retired from?" she asked.

"I was a soldier," Henry replied. "For almost thirty years. Now I'm not." He said it just a little more harshly than he meant it, and he smiled at Bonnie to take the edge off his words. "I've been out for about six months now."

"Where's your home?"

"I don't rightly know as I have one. When a fellow's moved around as much as I have, I guess you sort of give up on the notion of having a home."

"Don't you have any family?"

Henry shook his head. "Not really. My folks are dead. Been dead for years. I had a sister, but she got married while I was overseas. Married some fellow from up around Detroit."

Bonnie smiled shyly. "I like the way you talk."

"What do you mean?"

"Your talk. I like it. I guess it's the accent, the way you say things." She finished her Corona. "Hasn't anybody ever told you that before?"

"Never," Henry said. He grimaced and leaned back in his chair.

"What is it?" Bonnie asked, alarmed that she had said the wrong thing.

Henry shook his head. "Nothing, just a bit of a stomach-ache. Listen, can you get yourself home OK?" Before she could answer he lurched to his feet and handed her a twenty-dollar bill. "Here, pay for the drinks and use the rest for a cab." He hurried from the table and made it outside before throwing up, but just barely.

"How in the world did you find me?" Henry stood at the door of his rented bungalow with only a towel around his waist.

"It wasn't too hard," Bonnie said. "The bartender where we had drinks last night said he heard you had rented this place. Can I come in?"

"Sure. But the place is a mess. I'm not what you call big on housekeeping."

"Here," Bonnie said, handing him a small thermos container. "I brought you some chicken soup. For your stomach."

Henry took the thermos into the kitchen where he almost heaved at the thought of food, even something as benign as a bowl of chicken soup. "Thanks," he said, returning to the living room where Bonnie still stood. "Did you make it?"

"Make what?"

"The soup. Did you make it yourself?"

"Oh, yes." Bonnie nodded. "It's Campbell's. I heated it up."

Henry smiled. "Well, that's what counts. Look, I was just about to take a bath when you knocked. Why don't you relax out here, and after I get cleaned up we can go out for coffee or something."

Henry eased himself into the hot water with a sigh. Although the narcotic prescribed by the VA doctor had allowed him to sleep, it had not been a restful night. *Good Lord, vomiting in the street like some kid right out of basic training.* He was not amused. He rested his head on the back edge of the tub and closed his eyes. He thought about the bodybuilder being photographed on the beach. When he opened his eyes again Bonnie was standing beside the tub looking down at him.

"I thought I could scrub your back," she said.

When he didn't answer she unbuttoned her blouse and let it fall to the floor.

Breasts, Henry thought, startled at the sight. *God only knows how long it's been since I've seen a young woman's breasts.* "You're making a big mistake here," he said, shaking his head. "I'm unfortunately not in a position to be, uh..." He paused and decided to come at it from a slightly different angle. "My situation, what with the medicine I'm taking and all, is, well, means that I can't exactly, you know..." He shrugged, unable to say it. "Look, why don't you just put your shirt back on and wait for me out in the living room, OK?"

Bonnie reached down and picked up her blouse. She left the bathroom without saying anything. Henry quickly finished his bath and went into the bedroom to dress.

"There's a little coffee shop just a block from here," he called into the living room as he pulled his trousers on. "Why don't we walk up there, and I'll buy you some breakfast." He came into the living room buttoning his shirt with one hand

and holding his shoes with the other. "What do you say?" The room was empty.

Henry waited two days before going back to the grill where Bonnie worked. "I've still got your thermos," he said when Bonnie came to his table to take his order.

"Were you ever in Vietnam?"

Bonnie and Henry were drinking coffee out of paper cups as they walked along the beach.

"Two tours."

"I never knew anyone who was actually there before. Was it terrible?"

"Must not have been. I don't remember it that way."

"I thought everybody who went there hated it."

"You can't believe everything you hear."

"Weren't you afraid of dying?"

"I don't think so. Fact is, a lot of us who were over there enjoyed it. You don't think much about dying when you're nineteen or twenty. I was just glad the war hadn't ended before I got a chance to get into it." He smiled. "You asking me about the war just got me to thinking about how I left home." He shook his head, pleased with the fullness of his memory. "My old man had to get up early to take me into Smithfield so I could catch the bus to Raleigh. My mother was so annoyed that I had joined the army she wouldn't get up to see me off that morning. But the night before, she still packed me up a nice lunch to take along. I can tell you what it was, too: some fried chicken wrapped up in wax paper and a couple of pieces of white bread. You remember the damnedest things, don't you?"

"Is this an army tattoo?"

Henry felt Bonnie's finger tracing the faded blue outline of an oriental dragon that adorned a small portion of his left rear deltoid muscle. Several weeks had passed and they were sitting on the seawall near the Venice Beach volleyball courts. Henry smiled, thinking of the tattoo parlor in Washington, D.C., where he had gotten the tattoo. He had been en route to Vietnam, his first tour. For reasons he could no longer remember, he had stopped off in Washington on his way to Dover Air Force Base in Delaware. *What was her name?* he wondered. *Judy? Was Judy her name?* He'd met her in a bar in Washington the night he got tattooed. *The thing was*, Henry thought, *was the boy*. He'd never forgotten the boy.

"Hey, you got a kid," he'd said, startled at the sight of a small child sleeping on the sofa. They had gone directly to her apartment from the bar. "What if it wakes up?"

"It's a *he*," Judy had responded, somewhat testily, "and he won't." She picked up the sleeping child, laid him gently on the floor next to the sofa, and covered him with a blanket.

It was a miserable little apartment, one room and a kitchenette below the sidewalk, two miles from the White House. The sofa made into a bed of sorts, filling the small room. The boy, of course, woke up. Henry's heart had shriveled just the tiniest bit when his eyes met the boy's, peeking out from underneath the blanket at the strange man astride his mother. Later, as he dressed to leave, she asked him for money.

"It's not like I'm hooking or anything," she told him, "it's just that, you know, we could use a couple of dollars."

Judy was married and worked for a coal company in the District. She told Henry that her husband was a sailor, and she hadn't seen him for almost a year. Still, she said, she loved him, because he was always good to her and the boy whenever he was around.

"What's the boy's name?" Henry asked quietly at some point during the night.

Judy was getting up to go to the bathroom and didn't hear his question. "There's a beer in the fridge," she called out. "Help yourself."

He didn't ask again. When he left in the morning he gave her forty dollars, half the money he had in his billfold.

"What's that?" Henry realized that Bonnie had said something that required an answer. "What did you say?"

"I said, I'm thinking of getting a tattoo myself. What do you think of the idea?"

A sadness came over Henry as he thought about the name-less boy in Washington, D.C. He shook his head. "Not much. A tattoo's a sign of ignorance, pure and simple."

"But you've got one," Bonnie teased.

"Yes, and I'm ignorant."

How else to explain it? he wondered. *How else to explain a life spent in the barracks?*

Because of bad weather in Alaska it took him three days just to get to Japan, and there, while waiting for a flight out of Tachikawa Air Force Base to Vietnam, he discovered that Judy had given him a little something to remember her by. At the base dispensary the doctor, an old China hand, undertook to lecture him on his responsibilities as an American GI abroad.

"These people aren't like you and me," the doctor told him, assuming that Henry had contracted gonorrhea somewhere in the Orient. "They can't be trusted. You've got to be more careful," he said, holding Henry's penis rather delicately between his thumb and forefinger. "Do you get my point?"

An Air Force nurse, a captain from Des Moines, came into the small examining room several minutes later carrying two large, stainless steel syringes on a small tray. She didn't look happy.

"I'm not going to lie to you, sergeant," she told Henry. "These shots are going to hurt."

"Henry? I brought you some soup and a sandwich."

He woke slowly, drenched with sweat. "Mom?" He struggled to rise up on one elbow. "Mom, is that you?"

"Henry, it's me, Bonnie." She was suddenly frightened by the look of confusion on his face. "Don't you remember? I told you I'd bring you some food when I got off work. Are you OK?"

He sagged back down on the mattress, exhausted by the effort to clear his head of the narcotic-induced confusion.

"Yeah, yeah, I'm fine. It's the goddamn pills. Look, darling, light me a cigarette, will you?" He rubbed a hand across his face. "And bring me a towel."

"Cigarettes are bad for your health," Bonnie said, handing him a Camel.

Henry laughed, a short bark devoid of humor, and sat up on the edge of the mattress. "Jesus, I must have been asleep the whole time you were at work."

"Would you like to try and eat a little?"

His stomach turned at the thought of food. "What time is it?"

"Just after one." Bonnie undressed, letting her blouse and skirt slip to the floor next to the mattress. "Do you want anything before I get into bed?"

"No, thanks. I've got to get up anyway."

He rose slowly, rolling from the mattress into a squat and then pushing off his thighs with both hands to stand, his lower back aching from the exertion. In the bathroom, he threw the burning cigarette into the toilet, relishing the short-lived hiss of the dying ember. *What sound would represent my life?* he wondered, looking down as he made water. *What does a life sound like, in the end? What does it smell like, how does it taste?*

Back on the mattress he cuddled next to her, snugging his pelvis into her buttocks. He drew heat from her body, wicking it out of her in shimmering waves of energy that danced off the walls and broke back over them like the surf at Venice Beach. He could feel the presence of prior lovers and wanted badly to please them as once they had pleased him, to tell them what was in his heart, as once he hadn't dared. After a time, and without realizing it, he fell asleep, his slow, even breath warm on her neck.

He was a boy again, wandering alone through a deserted army base, a tidy, if rather dilapidated, world of oxidized white and faded olive drab army housing. Adjacent to the base, out of sight but not mind, was a cemetery, a national cemetery. The barracks, mess halls, and supply rooms of the base were boarded up and waiting for death with quiet resignation like the old veterans they had once served. He walked alone throughout the base, peering into windows and trying all the doors. With quiet wonder, unafraid, he stole through countless squad bays and orderly rooms, fascinated by the emptiness, touched in an inexplicable way by the passage of so many anonymous lives through the vacant and exhausted buildings. Many of the platoon and company bulletin boards still had official notices and orders thumbtacked to them, the yellowed onionskin summoning long-departed GIs to kitchen police and guard duty. At the adjacent cemetery, military funerals were conducted throughout the dream, the melancholy strains of "Taps" rising above the elms and sycamores, fading in and out as a cold wind blew across the dream's horizon.

Bonnie quit her job to be with Henry all the time. They spent the daylight hours on the beach, where the sun seemed to help keep the pain under control. Henry weakened as the days, or weeks, passed. He couldn't be sure which, because the passage of time had become no more than the wind-blown rustle of hamburger wrappers and paper cups along the seawall, as indistinct and formless as the gray people who shuffled along winnowing a living out of the municipal trash cans. When he needed help walking the three blocks between the beach and the rented bungalow, which was more often than not, he leaned on Bonnie and thought of the boundless strength he had known as a young man.

"Guns."

Bonnie looked up from her paperback. They were sitting on a blanket in the sand, regulars with a proprietary interest in their own little square of beach.

"What did you say?"

Henry nodded to his rail-thin right arm. It, like the rest of him, was tanned to an anomalous golden brown.

"Guns," he repeated. "I thought I'd always have the big guns."

Nights he spent with Percodans, sweating until the mattress was soaked and Bonnie had to dry him with one towel after another. She took to sitting up most of the night, watching him, listening to his rambling sleep-talk. Neither of them ate anything to speak of, and Bonnie's cheeks soon looked almost as gaunt and shrunken as his. She slept during the day, on the beach, her head lolled back in the sand, while Henry watched the waves roll in and wondered where his life had gone.

He thought of his father a great deal, and was troubled that he could no longer remember certain details of the old man's life. He realized with some bitterness that his memory was no longer his to command, that extraordinary recollections now hovered just out of reach, dissolving when he consciously tried to summon them, returning at the oddest times to startle him with their clarity, only to recede again, stealing away the names and faces of departed comrades-in-arms. He kept coming back in his mind to the last time he had seen his father, the morning the old man had driven him to catch a bus to join the army.

It wasn't much of a day, to tell the truth. Only a hint of dawn, no more than a promise, really, was evident when they pulled over at a little diner on the old county blacktop a mile or two out of Smithfield. The tentative light revealed a low, gray, undertaker's sky, umber clouds scudding along on a raw January wind. Breakfast was a quiet affair, the two of them looking in different directions, Henry forward, the old man back. At the bus station, while waiting for the bus, they sat in the car and shared a cigarette, each unwilling and therefore unable to speak. Finally, when the Greyhound arrived, Henry and the old man shook hands. Unable to tell his son that he loved him, the old man told Henry instead that he had had to hitchhike into Bluefield, West Virginia, when he had joined the army in 1923.

"But I believe I know now what he meant."

Henry spoke not to Bonnie, who, as usual, had fallen asleep next to him on the blanket, but to a nameless young man who had taken to sitting near them on the beach every day. Obviously non compos mentis, the youth rocked gently back and forth for hours at a time, never taking his eyes off Henry. It was clear from his filthy appearance and talonlike finger- and toenails that no one was caring for him. At first the lifeguards, feeling protective toward Henry and Bonnie, had wanted to roust him, but Henry, of all people, interceded. Contemptuous of long-haired hippies and anyone with a non-regulation approach to life when he'd had the big guns, Henry had lately discovered that the maintenance of expectations was simply too taxing.

"Hell, he's probably a veteran like me," he told Bonnie when she complained about the smell. "Besides, he'll keep the flies occupied and away from us."

The demented kid was the first one to notice when Henry died. He had been waiting, as he usually was, when Henry and Bonnie arrived at the beach that morning. He watched carefully, as a cat might, while they spread their blankets and settled down on the already hot sand. Bonnie pointedly ignored him, as she usually did, and concentrated on getting Henry settled comfortably next to her. That accomplished, she promptly fell asleep, her paperback book open and resting on her stomach. Henry smiled at the boy and gave him a thumbs-up sign, shifting his body restlessly on the blanket, waiting for the sun to relax his pain-tightened muscles. He finally drifted off to sleep, leaving the young man to rock silently back and forth on his haunches, a peripatetic lookout faithfully watching for cowboys, or Indians, or whatever. After an hour Henry woke briefly, smiled at Bonnie's fitful snoring, and looked over at the suddenly attentive young madman.

"That'll do," he murmured, and, just like that, he died.

Bonnie slept for another two hours until she was awakened by one of the lifeguards who'd noticed that the young man was crying, silent tears that streaked over his cheekbones and quickly disappeared into his raggedy, unkempt beard.

Jackson Street

Mary Alice Goodman taught piano and lived on Jackson Street, in a house that surely cried at night. The house, although well maintained and tidy, had begun to settle rather more heavily onto its foundation as if accepting, after no more than a short struggle, the futility of resistance to gravity and heartbreak. Mary Alice, too, had begun to settle somewhat. Loneliness followed her around the house like a cat, rubbing affectionately at her ankles during the day and sitting on her lap, purring, as she took her hair down before retiring for the night. No men with bouquets or boxes of candy came to call and, with her father seven years dead, no one sat on the front porch and told her how pretty she was. Truth is, folks around Johnston County spent precious little time thinking about Mary Alice, and when they did, they thought her plain-looking and proper, the way a piano teacher and a good Baptist ought to be.

I started doing yard work and running errands for Mary Alice when I was fourteen or fifteen. For that first year or two I didn't much get to know her—she told me what needed fixing or cleaning up and I did it. Over time though, particularly after my mother died and the old man took to drinking a little, we became friends. Often after I'd finished up one chore or another she'd have me stay over for supper. She wasn't much of a cook but she was sure enough better than the old man, and I loved to just sit and listen to her talk. She told me all about Atlanta, where she'd gone to music school, and how much she wished she could go to New York or even Europe. She played the piano for me occasionally, and even a fool would have seen how much emotion she had inside, all bottled up.

My cousin Virgil told me, much later, that she had had only one lover in her life before him, a professor at the school she went to in Atlanta. He was a married man, and I conjured up a vision of Mary Alice shrinking and drawing back in fear even as she was compelled to lie under him, eyelids fluttering in helplessness, pale hands too timid to caress. Unable to say no, ultimately she fled, riding the Greyhound home to begin her life sentence as a piano teacher. When I told Virgil about the way I thought it must have been for her he just laughed. "Don't count on it, sport," he said.

Nobody ever knew for sure why Virgil Green came back to Smithfield. Virgil and I were cousins on my momma's side, although he was a good ten years older than I was. I grew up thinking that Virgil was just about the best cousin a fellow could have. "Now don't you be telling your momma I taught you how to do this, you hear?" he'd say after giving me a pinch of his chewing tobacco or sharing a cigarette with me. He showed me how to throw a curve ball and how to fool a squirrel when you're out hunting, and all the big kids left me alone because Virgil and I were kin.

During his senior year of high school he got caught messing around with Jim Nance's wife. Jim was finishing up a five-year sentence for voluntary manslaughter at Central Prison over in Raleigh at the time, and so naturally quite a few people around the county knew about it before Jim did, what with Virgil loving to brag on himself and Jim's wife being a good-looking woman. When Jim finally found out, he vowed to kill Virgil at the first opportunity. Virgil heard of the threat and, considering the source, slipped permanently out of town one night shortly before Jim's release, breaking both his momma's and my heart.

I hated Jim Nance mightily after that, and when he was killed in an accident out on the interstate I felt that an old score had been settled. We heard first that Virgil had joined the army and a few years later that he was out in California. After his momma died we lost touch with him, and he gradually faded from most everyone's memory. Except mine. I never forgot him. Then, in the springtime of my last year of high school, just as the dogwood trees and rhododendrons were showing color, there he was, standing on our front porch. He told us he had heard that my mother had passed and wanted to let us know how sorry he was. The old man asked him where he was staying, and when he told us he wasn't rightly settled just then the old man invited him to stay with us.

Having Virgil around was like having a black-sheep uncle, an older brother, and a best friend all at once. He took to hanging around down at the American Legion hall where he could shoot pool and drink beer. Everybody liked Virgil, especially the old vets down at the Legion, and so naturally people started making up stories about him. Most folks remembered how he had made a fool of Jim Nance, and pretty quickly there was a rumor circulating as to how he had killed a man in California. Over a woman. Another story had him saving some officer's life in the army and a third allowed as how he had won a lot of money gambling and was just laying low in Smithfield until the heat wore off. Down at the Legion hall Virgil would merely lean against the bar and wink when someone would ask him about one rumor or the other, thereby confirming that all were true. Of course me and the old man knew there was nothing to any of it, but it made us both kind of proud anyway.

Mary Alice was quite concerned about my future that spring. She knew I was thinking about joining the army, and she spent numerous evenings trying to convince me to enroll at little Campbell College over in Buies Creek instead. As she talked I imagined us as lovers and indulged in countless fantasies woven about that supposition. I frequently worked myself into such a state of arousal that I was scarcely able to talk to her at dinner.

It was during the course of one such evening in late May

that Virgil stopped by to ask if I wanted to ride over to
Durham with him to watch the Bulls play Rocky Mount.
Looking back on it I realize that he really came by to get a
look at Mary Alice. I hadn't told her a great deal about Virgil, instinctively afraid, I imagine, that she might take some
interest in him. When I introduced them I noticed for the
first time that Virgil had a dimple in one cheek when he
smiled and that with women his smile was different, more
personal-like, than it was with men. His eyes changed subtly
when he smiled at her, the pupils dilating ever so slightly,
like he knew a little secret he just might share with her, but
not until later, when they were alone.

"Lord, Mary Alice," he told her, standing there in the
kitchen, "it's surely been a while, hasn't it?"

I could see that she was clearly flustered by his presence,
the too-familiar way he looked at her, and I felt a flash of jeal-
ousy.

"Hey, I've got an idea," he continued, as if the thought had
just popped into his head, "why don't the three of us go to
the ballgame together?"

I could tell right away that she wanted to go.

"No, thank you," she said, "I really couldn't."

Virgil acted like he hadn't heard her. "Tell you what," he
said, picking up a plate from the table, "me and Randy
here'll straighten things up while you get yourself ready."

The Bulls beat Rocky Mount three to two in ten innings,
and I never saw Mary Alice have so much fun.

The next two or three times I saw Mary Alice she asked
me about Virgil. She tried to make the questions seem harm-

less enough, almost as if she were repeating a silly rumor rather than asking a direct question.

"Mrs. Gibson," she would say, "down at the Piggly Wiggly, told me that your cousin Mr. Green"—she always referred to him as Mr. Green to me—"has the town quite in an uproar." Or, "Mr. Green has quite a reputation, wouldn't you say, Randy?"

Actually, I said very little. I knew what she wanted me to tell her, but I couldn't do it to save my life. After a couple of days she didn't ask anymore—and I knew that she had made up her mind to go out with him if he asked again. But Virgil was too smart for that. He let several days go by before he made up an excuse to come by her house again and then he didn't do more than tell her what a good time he had had at the ballgame. After that he came by a day or two later, "just for a cup of coffee," he said. She was different when he came around, in a way that infuriated and depressed me all at the same time. I can't really describe it other than to say she became suddenly vulnerable, softer somehow, more feminine. A way she never was with me.

Virgil borrowed the old man's Plymouth the next day and disappeared for a week. He told us he had to take care of some business over near Greensboro but never said anything about planning to be gone for so long. After two or three days Mary Alice asked me, very casually, if I thought me and the old man and Virgil might not like to come by for dinner one night. When I told her that Virgil had taken off with the old man's car and we didn't know when he was planning on coming back she got quite upset.

"Oh, my," she said, "what are you going to do?" I shrugged.

"The old man's not too worried," I said. "He figures Virgil has probably got himself a girlfriend somewhere." I said the last part with a certain hurtful glee, anxious that Mary Alice know how I felt about the whole thing without having to say so directly.

As soon as I saw the look on Mary Alice's face, though, I regretted it. She sort of sagged in her chair, as if having her fantasy pierced was more than she could bear. I knew how she felt.

"But I don't believe it," I added quickly, leaning forward, wanting to touch her, "I don't think Virgil has a girlfriend at all. I think his business at Greensboro's just taking a little longer than he planned."

Virgil never did say what he had done the week he was gone. He apologized to the old man for keeping his car so long, and, as far as Virgil was concerned, that was that. Two evenings after his return the old man suggested the three of us drive into town for a movie and some ice cream.

"I don't much feel like getting out," Virgil said, "but I think the two of you should go."

I didn't like the way he said it, slowly and deliberately, as if he had a plan he wasn't letting us in on, but since the old man really wanted to go there wasn't much I could do.

"You two have a good time now, you hear?" Virgil called out as we left.

We got back to the house about nine-thirty and Virgil was nowhere to be found.

"Probably just stepped out to stretch his legs," the old man yawned.

I knew right away where he was. "You go on to bed," I said, "I believe I'll take a little walk myself."

It was a beautiful evening, warm but not full summer yet, with just the hint of a breeze. Mary Alice's house was dark and quiet. I slipped silently through the yard to the rear, where her second-story bedroom window looked out on the backyard. At first I couldn't see anything, but then, in the glow of a cigarette, the pale outline of Virgil's naked torso stood out in the window against the darker background. He was leaning against the windowsill, and although I couldn't see his face in the dark I had the feeling that he was looking right at me. And smiling. As I watched, scarcely able to breathe, I saw Mary Alice's arms wrap themselves around his waist, her hands dropping out of sight below the sill. I heard Virgil chuckle, and I knew the dimple was dancing to life on his cheek. He flicked his cigarette out the window toward me, and, mesmerized, I watched it all the way to earth. When I looked up again the window was empty.

Virgil moved in with Mary Alice the next morning. For a couple of days no one saw much of either of them. Then, gradually, life returned to normal. Mornings Virgil'd lounge about on her front porch in his T-shirt and jeans, drinking iced coffee and smoking cigarettes. Later, in the heat of the day, he'd generally head on over to the cool darkness of the Legion hall. After about a week Virgil stopped by the house and offered to buy me a beer.

"We've sort of missed you over at the house," he said.

"Mary Alice's worried that maybe you're put out with the two of us."

I shook my head and mumbled "I just figured you two wanted to be let alone for a while."

"Let alone for what?" he asked.

I couldn't look at him. "You know," I said.

He laughed.

It didn't take long for the mothers of Johnston County to express their disapproval of the new living arrangements on Jackson Street. Within a week all of her piano students had canceled their lessons and Mary Alice was left high and dry.

"What are you going to do?" I asked her one evening after the three of us had finished eating and were sitting on the porch with glasses of iced tea.

She smiled and shrugged. She had let her hair down, and it was all I could do not to reach out and touch it.

"I'll tell you what we're going to do, sport," Virgil said. "We're going to borrow your daddy's car and the three of us, you, me, and Mary Alice here, are going down to Myrtle Beach for a week. What do you think about that?"

June and July came and went as softly and easily as if the days and nights had been carefully wrapped in gauze. I spent all of my waking hours with Virgil and Mary Alice, returning home only to sleep. We stayed up late every night, talking, laughing, playing games. No one, least of all me, thought of what would become of us. Virgil and Mary Alice seemed to have enough money to underwrite our modest entertainments, and I knew, in a vague sort of way, that I would have to join the army at some point in the future, just as I presumed that the two of them would get married and Virgil would get a job, but there seemed to be no reason to be concerned just then.

I know it sounds bad, but looking back on it I can't honestly fault Virgil for what he did. I was upset with him at the time, but I know for a fact that he never meant to hurt anybody, least of all Mary Alice. Virgil was like a big, old dog everyone wants to love and take care of. He would spend a few days at your house, then a few with the neighbor up the street, and then maybe nobody would see him at all for a while. You can't let yourself get attached to a dog like that. Nor a man neither. Not if you're a woman.

The first hint that things were breaking up came when he again borrowed the old man's Plymouth for three days. He told Mary Alice and me that he had to tend to some business out of town. It bothered Mary Alice that he wouldn't tell her what his business was but she had so little experience with men she wasn't sure what to do about it.

"What kind of business do you suppose is Virgil in?" she asked me point-blank after he left. All I could do was shake my head and shrug my shoulders.

After the first day he was gone I stayed away from Jackson Street, for it seemed that, without Virgil, Mary Alice and I only made each other nervous. Then, on the third day he was gone, I ran into a friend of mine downtown who happened to mention that another friend of ours had just the day before seen Virgil down at Carolina Beach with Wanda Morton.

"Wanda Morton?" I repeated, stunned. "From down at the Wachovia Bank?" Wanda was just a year older than I was and worked as a teller. Not thinking, I said, "Virgil was supposed to be out of town on business."

My friend laughed. "I wouldn't mind being in that kind of business."

When Virgil got back into town I thought I'd let a day or two go by before I went over to see him and Mary Alice. I figured that it wouldn't take long for word of Virgil and Wanda to get around and that some good Christian neighbor was bound to call Mary Alice with the news. Meanwhile a guilty conscience told me it was time to drive over to the army recruiting station in Raleigh and get things underway. I ended up spending two days there, taking all different kinds of tests and physical examinations. Even then, when I got back, I put off going over to see Virgil and Mary Alice, not wanting to get involved in their situation.

Finally, late one afternoon almost a week after Virgil had gotten back from the beach he came by the house. "Thought I better stop by and say so long to you and your daddy," he said, a big smile on his face.

"Where you going?" I asked.

"Oh, just down the road," he said. "You know me—can't stay in one place for too long. Probably head back to California."

Behind him, out in the driveway, I could see Wanda Morton sitting in a new Ford.

"What'd Mary Alice say?" I asked.

He shrugged. "We didn't talk about it much," he said. "Hell, boy, she knew all along we didn't have any sort of permanent thing going on," he added defensively. It was plain that all this talk about Mary Alice was making him nervous. "Anyway," he said, turning to leave, "you take care of yourself."

I put it off as long as I could, going over to see Mary Alice. Finally, I went over the evening before I had to report to the army. She was sitting at the kitchen table when I knocked on the back door. It had been a terribly hot day, hot and humid, and a fan was struggling to move the heavy air around the kitchen.

"I joined the army," I said. "I'm leaving in the morning."

The labored hum of the fan seemed to fill the small room. I hesitated for a moment, not sure what to say next. Through an open window, to the west toward Raleigh, I could see lightning.

"It's fixin' to rain tonight," I said. Mary Alice rose and walked silently from the kitchen. After a minute or two I got up and let myself out the back door. The sky had darkened considerably, and the air was heavy with the smell of ozone.

Vancouver

The Eastern Whisperjet shuttle from O'Hare to Raleigh-Durham released its brakes at 11:00 P.M. and shortly thereafter crossed the Ohio River at an altitude of twenty-seven thousand feet. There were only four passengers on board, two businessmen in first class and two uniformed servicemen back in coach. All three stewardesses sat up front with the businessmen, only occasionally glancing to the rear of the plane. Shortly after takeoff one of the stewardesses walked back to the two servicemen to ask rather peevishly if they would like something to drink. One was a sailor, going home for his first leave after basic training at Great Lakes. He wore his uniform like his youth, self-consciously, and he called the stewardess, hardly older than he was, ma'am, grateful for the little plastic cup of Coca-Cola she brought him. The other man, an army lieutenant, didn't say a word, responding only with a slow shaking of his head to the young woman's inquiry, which annoyed her so much that she spitefully refused to leave the first class section of the cabin thereafter.

The sailor, bursting with the garrulousness of a young man away from home, badly wanted to talk to his comrade-in-arms but he had learned enough in basic training to recognize an officer's uniform and so was afraid to initiate a conversation. Finally, unable to contain himself, the young seaman leaned across the empty aisle and ventured, "We should be getting there pretty soon now."

The lieutenant continued to stare silently into the black night.

Only momentarily discouraged, the sailor tried again, somewhat louder this time. "I said, we should be getting there pretty soon now."

The lieutenant turned toward the young sailor. "I'm sorry, did you say something to me?"

Suddenly fearful, now that the lieutenant had actually spoken to him, the sailor stammered, "No, sir, uh, I mean yes, sir. I just said that I thought we'd be landing soon."

The lieutenant looked at the sailor without responding, increasing the young man's nervousness. Finally he spoke, his voice flat and uninviting. "You don't have to call me 'sir.' Not anymore."

The sailor nodded and sank back into his seat with a sigh, not knowing what the lieutenant meant. Of course he had to call an officer "sir." He wished he could have another Coke, but he had no idea how to summon the stewardess, and he certainly didn't want to call attention to himself. He could hear, beyond the curtain separating the first class section from coach, the laughter of the two businessmen and the three stewardesses. Maybe one Coke was all you were supposed to get.

SCENE: *Tan Son Nhut Air Base, Saigon*. Lieutenant Robert Strunk has missed the civilian charter flight on which he was scheduled to depart the Republic of South Vietnam and is forced to wait for available Air Force transportation. The passenger terminal at Tan Son Nhut, built by the French after the Second World War, is a monument to empire, wide porticos yielding to soaring white plaster ceilings and marble floors. It is late afternoon when Strunk arrives from Bien Hoa, his starched khakis and duffel bag marking him clearly as one either coming or going.

"Excuse me, sergeant, I have orders authorizing me to take the first available transportation back to the U.S. Who do I need to check in with?"

Other than Strunk there appear to be only two men in the entire terminal, a pair of Air Force NCOs in fatigues sitting behind what had been a civilian airline counter.

"You're looking at him, sir." The senior of the two sergeants takes a copy of Strunk's orders and consults a flight schedule pinned to a metal clipboard. "I've got a MAC 141 to Clark in the Philippines leaving in less than an hour. You could take it and try for something from there. Or I have a 141 scheduled for departure in six hours for Elmendorf and Travis. My advice is to wait for that one, because Clark can be a real cocksucker to get out of on standby."

As the hours pass, the two sergeants amuse themselves by shooting rubber bands at the lizards, which seem to be everywhere. One man spots a particularly large one where the wall joins the ceiling some eighteen feet above their counter. Although they both try a number of times, neither can get a rubber band near enough to cause it to move. After watching their futile efforts for several minutes Strunk opens his duffel bag and takes out a service Colt .45 automatic. The two sergeants watch, wide-eyed, as he chambers a round and takes aim. Before he can fire, one of the sergeants speaks up.

"Jesus, sir, I don't think you can shoot that in here."

Strunk, puzzled, looks at him. "Why not?"

"Well, sir, I mean, this is a passenger terminal."

Strunk shakes his head, raising the pistol again. "Fuck that. This is Vietnam, isn't it?" He fires and the lizard disappears in an explosion of plaster.

The sergeants cover their heads and run out from behind the counter.

"I think I got him," Strunk says, turning to aim at another large lizard he sees on the ceiling, "but it's hard to tell." He fires again, and more plaster rains down. He looks at the two white-faced sergeants. "You guys want to give it a try?"

The sergeants look at each other and then back at Strunk. Both nod affirmatively. SCENE FADES.

A taxi driver, annoyed that he had dozed through the arrival of the last flight into Raleigh-Durham that night, hurried into the terminal. "Say, soldier, need a cab?"

The lieutenant looked at him. "How much to Smithfield?"

"Smithfield, Christ, that's way to hell and gone on the other side of Raleigh. I'll have to charge you twenty bucks to go out there. And look here, I'd like to help you with that duffel bag but I've got the bad back, you know what I mean?"

It was one-thirty in the morning when the cab got to Smithfield's two-block-long business district. The lieutenant indicated the darkened storefront of Trout's Drug Emporium.

"You sure this is where you want to go?" The cabbie examined his passenger in the rearview mirror, convinced that the stone-silent young man must be a Section 8.

The lieutenant got out of the cab without a word and carefully settled his garrison cap on his head before paying the driver and retrieving his duffel bag from the trunk. "Fuck you," he said quietly as the cab made a U-turn and sped out of town. He dragged the heavy duffel over to the bench sitting on the broad sidewalk in front of the drugstore's picture window. He noticed a dark shadow reflected in the window and stood looking at it for several minutes, unable to recognize himself. Finally he sat down on the worn bench and pulled a crumpled pack of cigarettes out of his pants pocket. The sudden flare of his lighter caused him to flinch involuntarily, a response that first annoyed and then amused him. One side of the lighter had his name engraved on it, *Lt. Robert Strunk,* above a tacked-on pair of miniature chromed paratrooper's wings. Unable to relax, he stood up and walked anxiously down the empty street, unconsciously skirting the wan cones of light thrown by the street lamps. The steel taps on his paratrooper boots sent the sounds of his footsteps reverberating past the darkened storefronts, and he wished that morning would never come, that he could remain forever alone in the still August night.

He had just returned to the bench when he heard the police car turn onto Main Street and drive in his direction. It stopped in front of the drugstore and a powerful flashlight beam centered on his face.

"What's your business out here this time of night?"

Shielding his eyes with the flat of his hand, Strunk smiled, pleased that he recognized the voice. It was Otis Ferguson, oldest of the three Ferguson boys. Strunk had gone to school with the youngest one, Tom.

"It's me, Otis, Bobby Strunk. Turn that light out, you're fixin' to blind me."

"No shit, is that you Bobby? What in the world are you doing back here? You home on leave?"

The patrolman got out of his car and walked gingerly up to the lieutenant, still unsure if he could believe his eyes and ears.

"Yeah, it's me, Otis. No, I'm not on leave. I've been discharged, finished my hitch. I'm just back from Vietnam."

"Well, goddamn, Bobby. What in the hell are you doing out here in the middle of the night? I got a call from the police over in Raleigh. They said a cabdriver called them to report that he had dropped a crazy man off in Smithfield. Said I should investigate."

"I just flew in and figured I'd wait here until morning and then get someone to give me a ride out to the house. I don't know if anyone's been looking after it since the old man passed. It was already so late I didn't think it made a lot of sense to get a hotel room in Raleigh. Say, if you don't mind, maybe you could run me out to the house now."

Otis shifted his feet and looked away for a minute. "Jesus, Bobby, we were all sorry about your dad dying, especially what with you being overseas and all." Otis paused and cleared his throat. "I'm afraid there's a slight problem about you going out to the house right away."

"What do you mean, problem?"

"Well, because you were away, old Judge Grover had to appoint what you call an executor to look after your dad's affairs until you could get home. And, since no knew for sure when that might be, the judge allowed the executor to rent the house out so it could generate some income to pay the bills."

"What bills?"

"Well, damn, Bobby, you know. It costs money to get buried properly, and legal fees for the estate, things like that. Hell, can't even a nigger die for free in Johnston County anymore."

"I guess not. Still, that sort of puts me at loose ends for a while. Who's this executor the judge appointed?"

"Some lawyer over in Raleigh—I forget his name. They can tell you at the courthouse tomorrow. Look here. You can come on down to the jail and sleep there if you'd like. Then tomorrow you can get yourself situated."

"Thanks, Otis, but if it's all the same to you I think I'd just as soon stay here. I'm thinking in the morning I'll catch the bus to Raleigh and get me a room. Say, how about the old man's Buick? Is it still around?"

"No, Bobby, I'm sorry. The judge ordered it sold. In fact they pretty much sold off everything except some personal things the lawyer has stored in Raleigh."

"How about the old man's dogs?"

"I'm afraid they're gone too."

"I'll be damned."

"Look, you can stay here if you want. The bus to Raleigh still comes through at seven-thirty."

Otis started to get back into his patrol car and stopped, remembering something he wanted to ask. "Say, Bobby, you heard about Tom didn't you?"

"Yeah, Otis, I got a letter from the old man."

"His company commander wrote a nice letter, only he didn't tell us much about how he died. I don't suppose you'd know any of the details, would you?"

"No, I'm sorry, Otis. We were in different units and in different parts of the country."

Neither man said anything for the longest time. Finally, Otis spoke. "Welcome home, Bobby."

SCENE: *The Carolina Diner in Smithfield*. Valgene Pendergraft, owner of the Esso station, is having a cup of coffee with Sonny Long, local realtor and notary public, and Deputy Sheriff Bill Beauchamp.

"I declare, Sonny," Valgene says, "I haven't seen hide nor hair of you for a right smart while."

"I had to take the wife over to Sanford to her mother's. I been back a couple of days but I been so durn busy I could scarcely draw a peaceful breath."

Bill Beauchamp speaks up. "Say, you know who got back into town last night, back from Veetnam? Young Bobby Strunk."

"I'll be damned." Valgene looks up from the biscuit he's buttering. "He home on leave?"

"No, he's done finished up his hitch and been discharged. And looka here. Otis Ferguson found him sitting all alone in front of Ed Trout's drugstore at two in the morning. Said he come into Raleigh-Durham and was just waiting until morning to get a ride out to his pa's place. Otis had to tell him about Judge Grover renting the place out. Anyway, Otis said he caught the seven-thirty Greyhound to Raleigh this morning. Said he was going to get a room and look into his pa's affairs."

"Well, shoot. I tell you, it's a durn shame that boy has to come home and can't even get back into his own house." Sonny waves at Nancy Gordon to freshen up his coffee. "What do you reckon he's going to do about a job?"

Before anyone can answer Shirley Ann Brown walks by outside. Three heads swivel as one and young Bobby Strunk is, for the moment, quite forgotten. SCENE FADES.

Without knowing why, Strunk found the transition from military to civilian life unsettling. Like a man obsessed with the nagging fear that he has forgotten to turn off the coffee before leaving the house, he worried that he was missing something. It was as if the end of his life as a soldier had come too soon, catching him unprepared. Raleigh turned cool and gray as late summer yielded grudgingly to autumn. October was gone before he even knew it was nigh. He was uncomfortable sleeping without a weapon within easy reach so he bought a pistol, an army model Colt .45 automatic, and kept it beside the bed, loaded, with a round in the chamber. Often, when he couldn't sleep, he would sit on the edge of the bed and hold the heavy weapon in his hands, loading and unloading it, sliding the cocking mechanism back and releasing it, relishing the oiled authority with which it chambered a round. It was too bulky to conceal comfortably on his person, so he bought a Smith and Wesson .38 revolver with an underarm holster. He liked the feel of it next to his body and began wearing it as casually as a T-shirt. He sat alone in his apartment, content to spend his days in the recent past, savoring old victories, anguishing anew over made mistakes and done deals. Again and again he relived basic training and AIT, OCS and garrison duty, felt the texture of army life, heard the music of army bands blowing across parade grounds. He had merely to close his eyes and the images of countless barracks and squad bays swirled about him, his feet unconsciously responding to the cadence calls of unseen drill sergeants. And always there was the 'Nam. His radio call sign, Redwing Four, rang in his ears, a part of wireless communications unbroken by ten thousand miles and four months.

December took Raleigh by surprise, a bitter cold front moving in and settling over the Piedmont like an unemployed brother-in-law. The weather suited Strunk, his disposition as frigid and colorless as the lowering sky. For Christmas he treated himself to another weapon, a Colt AR-15, the civilian version of the M-16 he had carried in the 'Nam. He saw it in the window of a gun shop and was unable to resist, knowing it would provide a tangible link to the dreams and recollections that were now the better part of his life. The only problem with the rifle was that, in accordance with federal law, it would fire only in a semiautomatic mode, a limitation that Strunk found unacceptable. The owner of the gun shop, after some hesitation, gave Strunk the name of a gunsmith out on the Raleigh-Durham Highway, Orville Mabry, saying that Strunk could talk to him about any modifications he might wish to make.

"It's a felony to possess a fully automatic weapon."

Strunk looked around the seedy living room. Other than two wooden chairs the only piece of furniture was a long workbench, which occupied most of the room, its maple top cluttered with rags, tools, and numerous firearms in various stages of disassembly. The sweet tang of lubricating oil and solvent filled the damp, chill room. The entire house, actually little more than a four-room shack sitting at the end of a short, potholed gravel driveway just off the three-lane highway, was apparently unheated. Seated behind the workbench, wearing a filthy fatigue jacket and a black watch cap, was the gunsmith. Ignoring the smith's unsolicited and hostile statement regarding the legality of automatic weapons, Strunk motioned with his thumb toward the other person in the room, a one-legged man sitting in one of the wooden chairs. "Who's he?"

The smith shifted a large wad of tobacco in his right cheek and spat in the general direction of a coffee can sitting on the floor, missing badly. "He's my brother."

Strunk pointed at the blue and white patch depicting a winged sword on the left shoulder of the fatigue jacket the smith was wearing. "Did you serve with the 173rd?"

The one-legged man spoke up. "No, I did. That's my jacket. What's it to you?"

Strunk looked at him. "I was with the 82nd."

The one-legged man stood up and hopped over, using a cane awkwardly for support. "Phu Bai?"

"Yeah. Phu Bai and Phuoc Vinh. I was in the 2nd of the '05." Strunk nodded in the direction of the missing leg. "Tay Ninh?"

"You got it: 2nd of the '03." He extended his hand. "My name's Mabry, Emil Mabry." He nodded toward the smith, still seated behind the workbench. "This here's my brother Orville. Folks call him Buddy."

Strunk shook the proffered hand. "Name's Strunk. Always pleased to meet a veteran." He turned to the smith. "Now. Can you modify it to full automatic?"

Buddy looked over to his brother, who nodded affirmatively, and then smiled at Strunk, revealing several missing teeth. "I think we can do some business together. Be expensive though." He spat, again missing the coffee can cuspidor. "Cost you a hundred dollars."

Strunk nodded. "Do it."

A week later Strunk returned to pick up the rifle. Emil broke it down on the workbench, taking obvious pride in his brother's work. "Looka here," he said, "this new sear assembly Buddy fabricated's better than the factory coulda done."

His brother, who by all appearances had not moved from behind the workbench or changed clothes since Strunk last saw him, scratched his nuts contentedly, basking in his brother's praise. "Shit," Buddy boasted, working vigorously on his chew, "that sumbitch'll grind 'em out all day long. You'll melt the barrel down before that sear assembly'll go. Want to take it out back and bust a few caps?"

Strunk took the rifle and nodded, pleased with the workmanship. "Won't somebody hear the automatic fire?"

Buddy shrugged. "Fuck 'em if they do. We test-fire into the drainage ditch out back all the time. Nobody'll say nothin'."

Strunk, planning to take the weapon out into the woods on his own, had already loaded five twenty-round magazines with .223 calibre military loads he had purchased earlier in the week. The three men walked out through the filthy kitchen into the backyard, stopping at the edge of a muddy drainage ditch. Strunk inserted a magazine, drew back the slide, and chambered a round. He fired the first five rounds in the single-shot mode, each bullet impacting into the opposite side of the ditch with a wet smack. After five rounds he moved the new selector switch Buddy had mounted to the full automatic position, and triggered the remaining fifteen rounds in two long bursts. The two brothers stood to his right rear and smiled at each other, noting with pleasure the practiced ease with which Strunk handled the weapon. Strunk ran through the remaining magazines quickly, pleased that there was no evidence of a tendency to jam or misfire, even when he fired the last magazine in one prolonged burst of twenty rounds. He turned to the two brothers. "I like it."

Emil beamed. "Knowed you would. There ain't no better gunsmith hereabouts than Buddy."

As they stood there, a large crow, disturbed by the gunfire, quartered across the fallow field beyond the drainage ditch. Still holding the AR-15 in his left hand, Strunk quickly reached into his coat with his right hand and grasped the .38 Smith and Wesson nestled under his left armpit. In one fluid motion he withdrew the revolver, turned, tracked, and fired at the crow, flying now perhaps fifty yards away. The bird stumbled in flight, as the steel-jacketed slug passed through its body, and fell to earth in a shower of black feathers. Strunk holstered the revolver and turned back to his two companions.

The brothers Mabry were dumbstruck. They had just witnessed something miraculous, a feat of marksmanship they would not have believed possible had they not seen it.

Strunk saw the looks they were giving each other. "Lot of luck in a shot like that," he said, almost to himself, as the three of them walked back to the house. "I doubt I could do it every time. Come on," he added, slapping Emil carefully on the back, "I'll buy you boys a beer."

The three men drove to a roadhouse out in the county that the brothers frequented. The one-story, unpainted cinder block building, its windows barred and water-streaked, sat uninvitingly behind an unpaved, rutted parking lot. The cinder blocks had absorbed moisture unevenly, giving the structure an unfinished look, its damp, gray walls blending seamlessly with the low winter sky. Inside, a row of worn booths lined the wall opposite the bar. At one end a small dance floor awaited the evening crowd, the jukebox darkened and silent. The waitress brought them a pitcher of beer and jar of pickled pigs' feet. Strunk passed on the pigs' feet and poured the beer.

SCENE: *The Officers' Club Annex on Fort Bragg's Division Road.* Located in a converted World War Two–vintage wooden barracks, the club's interior consists of one large room with a bar at one end. Small wooden tables and chairs are scattered haphazardly throughout, as are several quartermaster-issue leather sofas. One of numerous such club annexes dotting the post, it provides an aggressively masculine environment within which the division's junior officers can consume large quantities of alcohol at exceptionally modest prices, particularly during the frequent so-called happy hours.

On this particular evening, the company commander of Bravo Company, Captain William Brown, is holding forth addressing his four platoon leaders, a weekly chore

he feels is critical to the successful orientation and socialization of the young lieutenants entrusted to him. Billy
Brown is Regular Army and takes his responsibilities very
seriously, an attitude reflected in an unbroken chain of superior fitness reports filed on him by his various commanding officers. In two years (assuming he survives an
upcoming second tour in the 'Nam) he will almost certainly be promoted to major and assigned to the Command and General Staff College.

"Shit." Billy Brown wipes the back of his hand across his
mouth before lighting a cigarette. "You guys have got me
fucked up again." He pounds on the table in mock anger.
"Another round. You lobcocks aren't drinking. I'm not
going to be the only one leaving here drunk tonight."

Second Lieutenant Strunk, his company commander's
admonition notwithstanding, *is* drunk. And happy. Six
weeks out of OCS, three weeks out of jump school, there
is nothing he'd rather be doing than getting drunk with a
man like Billy Brown. None of the young platoon leaders
have yet been to the 'Nam, a serious disadvantage after
the third or fourth drink, when war stories become the
primary topic of conversation. Forced to listen in frustrated silence, the lieutenants are reduced to mental posturing (*I'd have blown his fuckin' head off*) and emphatic
reinforcement of points made by others (*Fuckin' A!*).
Many of the stories, although apocryphal, reinforce the
siege mentality that dominates the military's thinking regarding the war in Southeast Asia. The lieutenants pound
on the table, knocking over several drinks, and roar with

laughter. Lieutenant Strunk can think of no other place in the world he'd rather be. SCENE FADES.

"Now let me get this straight." Strunk looked across the table at the Mabry brothers, both of whom were gnawing on pigs' feet. "You're going to pay me a thousand dollars just to ride along with you?"

Emil wiped his mouth with the back of his hand and nodded. "That's right. All you have to do is ride shotgun."

Strunk looked at Buddy. "Tell me about the guy who's setting up the deal."

"Like I tol' you, name's Buck Jackson. I met him when I was in the joint. Most of the time Emil was in the army I was serving my own time. Buck knows all about bringing marijuana into Florida from South America or some goddamn place. He brings the stuff up to South Carolina, we meet him with the cash, and do the deal. Then me and you and Emil drive back here, and you walk away with a thousand bucks. How about it?"

"Why do you think you can trust this guy?"

Buddy laughed. "I don't trust nobody. That's why me and Emil want you to come along. After what we see'd out back of the house I figure you can take care of whatever might happen. Not," he added quickly, "that we expect anything to happen. It's just that a fellow can't be too careful these days."

"What are you going to do with the stuff once you get it back to Raleigh?"

Buddy grimaced, annoyed by the question. "That's for us

to worry about. I'd say a thousand bucks just to ride down to South Carolina and back is a pretty good day's pay."

Strunk was silent for a moment and then pointed at Emil. "How much you get every month for that leg?"

"Shit. Not enough to live decent without having a job, and who's going to hire a one-legged man? What the fuck am I going to do, hobble around some goddamn filling station pumping gas?" Emil leaned across the table. "Let me tell you something, Strunk. Nobody wants anything to do with guys like you and me, grunts who went across the pond. They just want to make like we don't exist, like the war don't exist. Everybody else has been sitting back here in Fat City while the likes of us has been getting fucked over. I leave my leg over in that stinking shit hole, and all I get for it is a pissant check every month from the Veterans Administration. Nobody calls up to see how I'm doing, nobody comes by to say 'Hey, Emil, can we help find you a job, help train you for something? Oh, and by the way, Emil, we sure appreciate what you done for us over there.' Fuck no." Emil slumped back, his sudden anger exhausting him. "Look. We'd like you to come along. Yes or no?"

Strunk finished his beer. "Why not?"

This heap *needs new shock absorbers*, Strunk thought as he bounced around on the back seat of the Mabrys' '59 Fairlane. The brothers had picked him up at his apartment just after dark and drove straight through to Dillon, South Carolina. Strunk insisted that they pay him half the fee in advance, five hundred dollars, and Buddy had rather irritably done so, taking the cash from a cheap vinyl briefcase he pulled out from under the front seat. Both brothers drank from a pint of Ancient Age bourbon as Buddy drove. In Dillon, Buddy turned onto the county road that led to Mullins, following detailed directions given to him when he set the deal up. Exactly two and eight-tenths miles past the Confederate War Dead Memorial in Mullins they were to turn left onto a dirt road and follow it for a mile and a half. At that point, precisely at midnight, the deal would be consummated. As the car passed the Confederate Memorial, Strunk rechecked his hardware. He had the big Colt automatic in the shoulder holster which normally carried the Smith and Wesson .38 revolver. The Mabrys had wanted him to bring along the AR-15 but he had refused, saying that unless they knew something they weren't telling him the Colt itself would be sufficient. He was wearing his army fatigue jacket and had placed three extra clips for the Colt in the left pocket, figuring that if someone was still shooting after three clips it most likely wouldn't be him. He leaned over the front seat to speak to Buddy.

"If we get there first and they come up behind us, make sure they turn their headlights off before the deal gets going. I don't want us standing in the light and them in the dark. Then, when you and Kenny move forward to exchange packages I'll wait back at the Ford so I can have a better view of what's going on. If you hear me yell I advise you to drop down and low crawl to the side of the road."

"There ain't no need to worry about shit like that," Buddy responded, studying the car's odometer intently. "Buck won't be tryin' nothin' funny. He tol' me that he wants to do business with us for a long time."

Yeah, Strunk thought, *and you dickheads are paying me a thousand bucks to come along because you like my company.*

The dirt road was right where it was supposed to be, and the Fairlane turned left on schedule. At a mile and five-tenths Buddy stopped and turned off the lights and engine. "We're a few minutes early," he said, and took a drink from the almost empty pint of bourbon. "Where are you going?" he asked as Strunk started to get out of the car.

"I've got to drain my lizard," Strunk replied. Several minutes later, after adjusting himself comfortably inside his trousers, Strunk leaned down and tapped on the driver's side window. Buddy rolled it down and cocked his head outward. "Listen up. When your friends get here I want you two to go ahead with the deal as if I weren't here. I'm going to stay back, away from everyone, where I can see what's going on. If everything goes OK, let them leave first. You got that?"

Buddy nodded silently, clearly spooked now that his big deal was about to go down. As Strunk looked back down the arrow-straight road, he could see, more than a mile away, the approaching headlights of an automobile. He took a last look at the two brothers. "Unless this is the county sheriff I'd say your friends are right on time. Remember, first thing you do is get them to turn those headlights off so I can see what's going on."

Strunk walked to the front of the Ford and crouched down next to the grill. He reached into his jacket and pulled out the

Colt, checking one last time to make sure that a round was chambered and that the safety was off. The approaching automobile pulled up behind the Mabrys' Ford and stopped, its high beams limning the two brothers sitting inside. Four men, two of them carrying shotguns, got out. Strunk, hidden in the darkness, cocked his head, his concentration broken by the startling clarity of a suddenly recalled radio conversation with his battalion commander in Vietnam.

"Redwing Four, this is Roadrunner Six, over."

"Six, Four, over."

"Redwing Four, this is Six. What's your status? Are you in contact, over?"

"Six, Four, that's a negative, over."

"Redwing Four, this is Six. What is your present position, over?"

"Uh, Six, this is Four. Wait one, over."

Buddy Mabry got out of the Ford and walked nervously to the rear, one hand shielding his eyes from the other car's headlights. "Buck, is that you? Hell, boy, turn off them goddamn lights. I can't see a thing."

One of the men reached inside the car and turned off the headlights but left the parking lights on, dimly backlighting the four men now standing opposite Buddy.

"Yeah, it's me," Buck answered. "Who the hell else would it be? Who's that in the car?"

"Hell, Buck, that's just my brother Emil. Speakin' of that, who all you got with you? I thought it was just going to be us."

"Tell your brother to get out where we can see him."

"Yeah, sure, Buck, sure. Hey, Emil, come on back here." As his brother got out and hopped back using the side of the Ford for support, Buddy began talking again. "Now, how are we going to work this, Buck? Did you bring the stuff?"

"Yeah, everything's fine. Did you bring the money?"

"Hell yes, we brung the money. I said, didn't I?"

"Get it out here where we can see it."

"Redwing Four, this is Roadrunner Six. What is your status, over?"

"Six, this is Four. We're stopped about a klick from Hill 408, over."

"Redwing Four, this is Six. Why stopped, over?"

"Six, this is Four. We've got dense undergrowth on both sides of the trail. I'm trying to locate an alternative route to 408, over."

"Redwing Four, this is Roadrunner Six. Negative on alternative route. I want you up that trail ASAP, do you copy, over?"

"Six, this is Four. Copy trail. Out."

Buddy walked back to the rear of the Ford with the briefcase. He sat it down in the gravel at his feet. "OK," he said, trying to keep a note of confidence in his voice, "let's see the stuff."

One of Buck's men walked around to the passenger side of their automobile and pulled out a large suitcase. He put it on the ground between the two cars and knelt down to open it. While everyone was concentrating on the suitcase, Strunk, in an effort to improve his own view, crabbed side-

ways to his right, intending to inch up the side of Buddy's
Ford. As he moved, his right foot slipped on the loose
gravel. Buck's head jerked up at the unexpected sound.
"What the fuck?" He jumped to his left and saw Strunk squat-
ting next to the Ford's left front wheel well. "It's an am-
bush!" he yelled, reaching inside his jacket for a pistol.

Buddy immediately threw both his hands up and
screamed, "Don't shoot, for God's sake, don't shoot."

Strunk reacted without conscious thought when he saw
Buck reach into his jacket. In less than a heartbeat, he stood
up to gain a clear field of fire while raising, aiming, and firing
the heavy Colt. The first round caught Buck just above the
right eye. As Buck died, his two shotgun-carrying companions, unable to see Strunk, both fired at Buddy. Two charges
of .00 buckshot struck him simultaneously, cutting his body
nearly in half. Emil, in the sudden terror of seeing his
brother cut down forgetting that he had only one leg, leaped
away from the Ford and immediately fell sprawling in the
gravel. As he flopped on the road like a dog with a broken
back the shotgunners, still confused as to who had shot Buck,
swung their barrels in his direction, the ejected shells from
the rounds that had killed Buddy still in the air as the second
volley reverberated across the dark South Carolina countryside. The big Colt recoiled three more times as Strunk
smoothly swung the barrel from right to left. The shotgunners, deafened by their own blasts, never saw the man who
killed them.

"Redwing Four, this is Roadrunner Six, do you copy, over?" Road-runner, the battalion commander, had been trying repeatedly to raise Strunk on the radio.

"Six, this is Four, over."

"Redwing Four, this is Six. Are you still in contact, over?"

"Six, Four, negative, over."

"Redwing Four, this is Six. State your casualties, over."

Strunk looked around as he waited for the medevac chopper. A shitpot load, he thought, a shitpot fucking load.

Strunk stood between the two automobiles, the six bodies sprawled in the gravel at his feet. He knelt down and put a hand on Emil, thinking that he looked particularly forlorn lying there with only one leg. "Well, friend, you sure as hell traveled a long ways from Tay Ninh to die on this dirt road." Strunk paused and sat down next to Emil's body, feeling scoured out and empty, the automatic still in his right hand. He sat there for close to an hour, talking to himself and listening for the sound of helicopters. Finally he got up, stiff and cold, and considered his situation. The Fairlane was too badly shot up to risk driving. The rear window had been shattered, the left rear tire was flattened, and numerous buckshot holes had ravaged the trunk. Although Buck's car was untouched, Strunk was unsure how well it might be known locally and in any event was loath to get in and drive it. In the end he simply started walking down the gravel road toward Mullins. He got a ride almost as soon as he hit the county blacktop. An old black man driving a pickup truck stopped and asked where he was going.

"Up towards Dillon," Strunk answered evasively, climbing in.

"Well, I'll carry you as far as Fork," the old man said, pulling back onto the road.

Neither man spoke again for several minutes until Strunk pulled out his cigarettes and offered one to the driver.

"Thanks."

Strunk leaned over and lit the cigarette with his Zippo, looking carefully at the other man's lined face in the sudden flare. "You live in Fork, do you?"

The old man didn't take his eyes off the road. "Borned and raised. You're not from around here. You a soldier?"

Strunk nodded. "How'd you know?"

"Oh, I just knowed. My boys was both in the army. Out now, and livin' up north." The old man looked over at Strunk. "Where'd you say you was goin'?"

"I'll give you two hundred dollars if you'll drive me up to Raleigh," Strunk said by way of reply.

"Cash money?"

"Cash money."

"Let me see it."

Strunk laughed. "You don't think I got it?"

"Man be a fool to drive all the way to Raleigh and not see the money first."

Strunk reached into his pants pocket and drew out the five hundred dollars Buddy had given him just a few hours earlier. "There's more'n two hundred here. Good enough?"

Strunk slept most of the way, swaying with the motion of the pickup as it worked its way north. He woke up when the old man stopped for gas in Lumberton. "You ever been to Vancouver?" he asked as they pulled out of the filling station.

The old man shook his head. "Never heard of it. Around here?"

"No, it's out west. Friend of mine from the army used to be from there. He was married."

The sun beat them to Raleigh, but just barely. Strunk had the old man drop him off at the Greyhound station. Before getting out he handed him the entire wad of cash from his pocket. "There's five hundred dollars there. Just in case somebody asks, you never saw anyone on the road, OK?"

The old man looked first at the money in his hand and then back at Strunk. "My boys was both soldiers," he said, his age-yellowed eyes inscrutable in the soft light of dawn.

Bethune, South Carolina

Barbara Johnson was the first Catholic girl I had ever known. Based upon rumors circulated in Baptist Sunday schools, I imagined her taking part in Latin rituals as fantastic and arcane as the Klan gatherings I had occasionally spied upon as a boy in Johnston County, North Carolina, heart pounding and eyes as big as silver dollars. It was September 1965, and she was a freshman at Duke, back when college girls still dated soldiers. She and her roommate, a girl from Spartanburg who was seeing a squadmate of mine named Danny Carter, drove down to Fort Bragg to watch one of the Hollywood jumps the division occasionally put on for visiting dignitaries and the folks back home. After the jump Danny and I big-timed it for the girls, dusty fatigues redolent with the sweet smell of burnt castor oil from the C-130s, Zippo lighters and Lucky Strikes, eyes shining and cheeks flushed.

At the end of the day, I made a date to see Barbara the following Saturday in Durham. We did little more on that first date than sit in the large reception area of her dormitory and talk. Although the conversation was somewhat strained, our lives touching on too few common points to allow shared values or interests, we nonetheless agreed to see each other again the following Saturday, both of us wondering, I'm sure, why. Our second date began, as our first had, with small talk in the dormitory reception area, but ended with Barbara sitting on my lap under a sycamore tree not far from the dorm asking me rather urgently not to ejaculate inside her. Afterwards, we sat on the stone wall that guarded the Women's Campus and shared a cigarette, as the whistle at the Erwin Cotton Mill across the street signaled the end of the second shift. I didn't find out what ejaculate meant until the next day, when I borrowed the first sergeant's dictionary and looked it up.

Without giving it a great deal of thought I became a Saturday night regular at the Rebel Yell Motor Court on the Durham–Chapel Hill highway. The owner, Buster Mason, was a disabled veteran of the Second World War with a Screaming Eagle and the barely legible words *Ste.-Mère-Église* tattooed on his right forearm. As a measure of his support for a strong America he gave me what he called the armed forces rate, five dollars and fifty cents a night, fifty cents off the civilian rate. He always had a chew going and kept a small Dixie cup in his shirt pocket into which he spat when he was indoors. He courteously offered me his plug of Brown Mule once, and I told him that although I did enjoy a chew every now and then I preferred Red Man or Beechnut to cut plugs. He told me that he once heard of a fellow who discovered a human thumb embedded in a plug of tobacco. Said he sure wished he could have seen that.

By leaving Fort Bragg as soon as possible after Saturday morning motor stables and inspection in the ranks, I generally made it to the Rebel Yell by one o'clock. Buster kept a case of Miller's chilling in the back of the Coke machine and usually insisted that we drink a couple before collecting my money and giving me a key. Barbara and I would spend the rest of the afternoon and evening cloistered in one of the tattered and ridiculously out-at-elbow cabins, door locked and shades drawn, cast-iron bed frame noisily protesting our otherwise silent couplings. She was always passive, accepting me with little outward enthusiasm yet never denying, never complaining. (Once, early on, she asked if I would like her to fellate me. Trapped without the first sergeant's dictionary for guidance I cautiously nodded assent. She must not have enjoyed it overmuch, for she never asked again.) As much as anything I remember the wonderful silence, the hours spent lying next to each other as the light faded inexorably away, leaving only the filtered neon glow of the Vacancy sign to pierce the gloom, a low-rent aurora borealis dancing over the bed. Back at her dorm, our good-byes were mostly limited to a confirmation of the desire to meet again the following weekend. Sunday mornings I'd get up early and steal away to Fayetteville, unsure of whether or not this was how things were supposed to be. By Monday reveille,

Saturday was no more than a vaguely titillating memory, as faded and colorless as Buster's tattoo.

"I'm pregnant."

I was not so much surprised as resigned, having grown up knowing that marriages generally got started in roadside tourist courts or the back seats of '49 Fords.

"I asked you not to ejaculate inside me."

Ignoring what I assumed was an essentially rhetorical accusation, I stated the obvious: "I guess we'll have to get married."

Like shadowboxers dancing in a darkened ring we began to spar, feinting and jabbing, bobbing and weaving, moving in separate spheres, each unaware of the other's words.

"A girl at the dorm knows an intern at Duke who'll take care of it."

I felt a heavy, although not yet uncomfortable, sense of adultness, of responsibility. "I'll take two weeks' leave, and we can drive up to Michigan so I can meet your folks. We could even get married up there if you'd like."

Barbara sighed. "The only problem is money. He wants five hundred dollars to do it."

I looked at Barbara. "Or we could get married at Fort Bragg. That way it wouldn't cost us hardly anything."

Barbara sat on the bed and hugged her knees to her chest. "Can you get five hundred dollars?"

I shook my head, puzzled. "Five hundred dollars? What in the world for?"

"**Now** let me get this straight," Danny Carter said deliberately. "This bitch wants *you* to come up with five hundred dollars to take care of *her* problem?" Four or five of the guys were gathered around my bunk in the squad bay, listening as I explained why I needed the money. They laughed.

Danny spoke again. "Now ain't this something? It may not even be your kid. Have you thought of that? Man, you need to tell her to fuck off, but quick." He lit a cigarette and glanced around at his audience. "My motto has always been 'Drop your load and hit the road.'" More laughter.

"Hey, come on man," I said, "I've got to do something. I can't just walk away."

Danny grabbed his crotch. "What you better do is get down to the dispensary for a short arm inspection to make sure she hasn't given you a dose of the clap."

As everyone drifted away, cheered by the realization that for once someone else's problem seemed worse than their own, I sat on my footlocker and despondently began spit-shining my jump boots, depressed by the knowledge that I had no more chance of raising five hundred dollars than the man in the moon.

Unseen, someone stepped up behind me. "Have you got a hundred dollars?"

Startled, I turned around.

Bill Robey was a weasel-faced little bastard from Bethune, South Carolina. He was short, not more than five foot six or seven, with scarred, lumpy hands and small feet. His nose, save for a single defiant protuberance midway down its length, lay at an unseemly angle against his face. He had bad teeth and a mean disposition that he wore like a pinkie ring, a walking challenge to anyone, drunk or sober, who might be inclined to fuck with him. Few were. He sat down next to me on the footlocker.

"Have I got a hundred dollars?" I repeated his question, not immediately connecting it with the group discussion that had just taken place.

"Didn't you just say you needed five hundred dollars to fix your girl's problem?"

I nodded affirmatively, repelled by the fetid smell of decay on his breath.

"I can get the job done for a hundred dollars."

What the fuck, over. I hadn't exchanged more than fifteen words with Robey in the past six months, and here he was offering salvation for only a hundred dollars. "How?" I wanted to know.

"First," he responded, "do you have a hundred dollars?"

I nodded again. His lips spread into a thin smile that the rest of his face refused to acknowledge. He leaned in closer and began to explain, his dark, hooded eyes holding me transfixed, his words at once frightening and exciting.

Barbara set everything up. I was to pick her up at the dorm on Saturday morning and drive her to the Hotel Durham, a three-story monument to changing times and hard luck across the street from the Greyhound bus station. We were to go to room 12 on the second floor, pay the money, and get the job done. Afterwards I would take her back to the dorm, and presumably that would be that. I didn't need Robey to tell me not to say anything to Barbara about the change in plans, figuring, number one, she already had enough to worry about and, I kept reminding myself, number two, it was my goddamn money.

As I had hoped, her preoccupation was such that she didn't notice Robey sitting in the back seat until we were actually in the car and pulling out of the parking lot next to the dorm. Explaining that he was the friend who had helped me with the money, I drove off immediately, hoping to forestall any protracted questioning. Robey said nothing beyond a polite "How do?" when I introduced him. Barbara began weeping quietly as we drove across town, holding her hands in front of her face. I felt sick to my stomach, wanting to comfort her but unable to do more than concentrate on the road, hands glued to the wheel. In the back seat Robey sat calm and serene, smoking a cigarette as he gazed out the window.

The desk clerk knew what we were there for. He didn't say anything, but he knew, his leering eyes an accusation broader than words.

"What are you looking at, dick-face?" Robey paused at the counter just long enough to intimidate the clerk, his dominance complete when the young man looked away and quickly mumbled an apology.

I gripped Barbara's arm tightly as we climbed the stairs to the second floor, assaulted by the odor of stale urine and vomit. Robey was smiling, humming a tuneless song, his brief encounter with the desk clerk having pleased him no end. We stopped at number 12 and knocked quietly on the door. "Who is it?" Robey nodded at Barbara, and she haltingly identified herself. Neither Robey nor I made a sound. The door opened just enough for us to see an eye, part of a nose, and half a mouth. In less than a heart beat Robey was in the room, slamming its sole occupant against the wall opposite the door. I quickly followed, dragging Barbara, and closed the door behind us. "Are you the doc?" Robey's voice was different, thicker and lower, and carried a chilling undertone of menace. A black, pebbled-leather physician's bag sitting on the bed left no doubt that we were in the right room. Robey abruptly slapped the doctor across the face, open-handed and very hard. A scant second later Robey struck again, the impact of his blow causing spittle to fly from the doctor's mouth as his head jerked to the side. Dread filled the tiny room. A knife blossomed in Robey's right hand, and he moved, reptilelike, over the slumped figure of his victim. He gripped the doctor's throat with his left hand and placed the point of the knife just under his right eye. A short, one-sided conversation followed, as Robey spoke in a sibilant whisper that neither Barbara nor I could make out.

Barbara clutched her rosary beads and hyperventilated, sucking in great mouthfuls of air, unable to comprehend what was happening. I quickly moved between her and the violence taking place against the back wall. Out of the corner of my eye I saw Robey take the knife from the doctor's face and help him roughly to his feet. For an instant the four of us stood silently looking at each other, strangers caught up in someone else's nightmare. Finally, an impatient Bill Robey snapped his fingers loudly to get the doctor's attention and then handed him his bag, saying brusquely that it was time to get started. As the doctor organized the remorseless instruments of his trade, lining them up on a towel spread at the foot of the bed, he indicated, more with gestures than with words, that he wanted Barbara to disrobe and lie down on the bed. When Barbara began to undress I looked over at Robey and motioned with my thumb toward the door. He shrugged and said he would wait just outside, looking pointedly at the doctor as he spoke.

The procedure itself was short and painful. I sat on the bed and held her hand, trying not to look and yet morbidly fascinated, unable to reconcile the wonderfully indolent afternoons at the Rebel Yell Motor Court with such unpleasantness. As Barbara moaned, I giggled nervously, thinking, *Here's another fine mess you've gotten me into!* The doctor looked up from between her thighs, amazed, I suppose, that I was laughing. Rather than meet his startled gaze I looked up at the water-stained ceiling, biting my lip to keep from smiling. It was like seeing someone stub his bare toe against a footlocker in the squad bay—you know it must hurt like a sonofabitch but you can't help laughing. Fortunately, the operation ended shortly thereafter, and I helped Barbara get dressed as the doctor explained what was going to happen in the next twelve hours. It didn't sound like the most pleasant thing in the world.

"*Raleigh, Smithfield, Goldsboro, Kinston, and New Bern.*" The loudspeakers at the bus station across the street were announcing departures as Barbara and I walked slowly to the Plymouth. I bent down to help her swing her legs up and into the car and felt a sudden sympathetic twinge of pain in my scrotum. *Goddamn*, I thought, *what's keeping Robey?* He had sent us on to the car saying that he wanted to take care of business (he pronounced it *bidness*) with the doctor. Leaving Barbara in the car, I walked back up the stairs and down the hall, wondering just how many business transactions such as we were concluding had been undertaken in the sanitary confines of the Hotel Durham.

Robey was coming out of the room just as I got there. "I hate a smart motherfucker, I swear I do," he was saying to no one in particular. Through the open door I could see the doctor lying on the floor, his face battered and bleeding.

"Jesus Christ, Bill, you didn't hurt him too bad, did you?"

Robey laughed and handed me a twenty-dollar bill. "Fuck him. Here. He had forty dollars on him. Our deal was for the hundred bucks you already paid me, so I'll split what he had on him with you." He looked back into the room and suddenly spat on the groaning, still supine, doctor. "I hate a smart cocksucker," he repeated truculently, hitching up his pants.

I tucked the twenty into my shirt pocket. Back at the dorm I told Barbara I'd phone her the next day to make sure everything was OK. After dropping her off, Robey and I bought a six-pack of beer and drove back to Fayetteville.

I never did phone Barbara. Every time I started to call, I froze up, knowing that there were no right words to say, no easy way to make her feel better. It would have been like getting a postcard from the beach: "Having a great time, wish you were here." Yeah, right. Fuck you.

Years later, after I was out of the army and working for a welding supply company in Charlotte, I passed through Bethune on a sales trip to Camden, South Carolina. Stopping for lunch, I told the waitress that somebody I knew from the army came from thereabouts, a fellow named Bill Robey. I asked if she knew him.

"Robey, Robey," she mused. "They used to be some folks name of Robey lived just outside town, but I believe they either up and died or moved away. Look here, sugar, you want that barbecue sliced or minced?"

Men

〜

I was eight when Daddy took up with a woman from Chapel Hill. It was the summer of 1959, and he was gone two days before Momma and I knew we'd been left. Not exactly a regular worker, Daddy often disappeared for a day or two at a time, fishing or hunting with one friend or another. Momma was just beginning to worry when a neighbor lady let on she didn't think he was planning on coming back. For the longest time I didn't know what Momma and I had done wrong.

We lived in town, in a little frame duplex on Hillsborough Road, two blocks from the insane asylum. The Harrises lived next door, in the other half of our duplex. They were an older couple who had had a son late in life. The son, Roscoe, was kept at the County Home over near Camp Butner. Mr. Harris worked at the Erwin Cotton Mill and came home from work every day covered with a fine cotton lint. Mrs. Harris stayed home and, after Daddy left, taught me how to read and make little animals out of broom straw. She drank paregoric and vanilla extract and had the sweetest smelling breath.

Mary Frances Mallinger was my best friend and lived across the street. Her daddy, everybody called him Doc, drove a bus for the city and was mean when he got to drinking. He was a paratrooper during the war and had tattoos on both of his forearms. Mary Frances and her mother, Irmaline, would hide over at our house when Doc was drunk and looking for trouble.

Doc Mallinger died not long after Daddy left. Momma said Doc drank himself to death, and I didn't doubt it. One of the Culp boys found him sprawled on the sidewalk in front of his house. Said Madison Green's hound was peeing on the body when he found him. Said he figured Doc was either dead drunk or just plain dead. They took the body to Creech's Funeral Parlor, over on Mangum Street. Irmaline told Momma that Doc had a five-hundred-dollar life insurance policy from the bus company and that she spent all of it on his casket. I think if you bought the most expensive casket Mr. Creech threw the funeral in for free. When Momma told the Harrises about it, Mr. Harris shook his head and said they should have just buried Doc wrapped in an old blanket and kept the five hundred dollars for more important things. Mrs. Harris hushed him and said men don't understand such things.

Momma couldn't come to the funeral because she had to

work. I was excited about going because I had never before seen a dead person. At the funeral parlor the five-hundred-dollar casket was sitting on a low platform, tilted so you could see the top half of Doc's body. As the service was about to start, Mr. Creech escorted Irmaline and Mary Frances up to the casket for a last look. Irmaline leaned over and laid one of her hands on Doc's face.

Suddenly, as if struck by lightning, she straightened up and began shrieking, "He's not dead, he's not dead!"

Before Mr. Creech could react, Irmaline reached in, grabbed Doc under the arms, and began pulling him from the casket. Mary Frances started wailing and leaped forward to lend her mother a hand. A stunned Mr. Creech finally moved in, in an effort to prevent them from removing Doc from the casket completely. Too late. Even as Mr. Creech tried to restrain Irmaline, Doc's legs and feet slithered free of the casket and the four of them—Irmaline, Mary Frances, Mr. Creech, and Doc—toppled to the floor.

I never did get to see the funeral. Several of Mr. Creech's assistants, alerted by all the commotion, came out and pulled a curtain across the front of the room. Everyone was asked to leave, and a private funeral was held the next day. Shortly thereafter Irmaline took Mary Frances to live with family in Murfreesboro, a place so far away as to have been on the other side of the moon as far as I was concerned.

Virginia Beach

It was the first week of April when Jimmy Mangrum's mother left
Jimmy with me and the old man and moved to Raleigh. She
had fallen crazy in love with a married Greyhound bus driver
from Ahoskie who got her a room and a job at the Carolina
Hotel, just across the street from the bus station. It was the
second blow in just under a year for Jimmy, since his daddy,
Turley Mangrum, had run off to Charleston with a nineteen-
year-old waitress from Fuquay-Varina not ten months earlier. It wasn't so much that Jimmy's mother wanted to leave
him behind, it's just that her new man told her he already
had two kids and wasn't studying taking on another. I guess
she figured that since Jimmy was almost seventeen (he was
just two months older than I was) it was time she listened to
her heart, and her heart told her Raleigh. I couldn't much
fault her, and although Jimmy was somewhat embarrassed

about the whole thing I think he understood. The old man, as usual, kept his own counsel.

Jimmy's mother hadn't been gone to Raleigh much more than a month or two when his daddy rolled back into town. Jimmy and I heard from Percy Inman, over at the Piggly Wiggly, that his daddy was back and asking about him. Percy was some sort of kin to Jimmy's daddy. Not enough kin to want to take Jimmy in when his mother left, but enough to where he could put on the dog for me and Jimmy.

"Yeah, I see'd Turley not two hours ago," Percy said casually, removing a nonexistent piece of lint from the front of his produce apron. "He was asking about you and your momma." Percy paused and rather indelicately sucked some air through his teeth. "I had to tell him about her moving to Raleigh."

Jimmy was too excited to get annoyed with Percy. "Did you tell him I was staying with Pete and his grandfather?" he asked.

Percy looked at me like I was a fly walking across the cut melons displayed behind him. "I did," he said. "Oh, and, uh, something else. Your daddy brung that girl back with him. The one from Fuquay. Left her out in the car while we was talking." Percy paused again, obviously enjoying the telling. "I believe she was feeding the baby."

"Baby?"

"Hell yes, boy, you didn't know?" He knew damn well Jimmy didn't know about any baby. "You got yourself a brand new baby brother."

A week passed, then two. We heard that Jimmy's daddy

had rented a house out on old Highway 70, up towards Wilson Mills. Jimmy was beside himself, not knowing whether his daddy was going to come see him or what. The summer days bled one into another, and still no Turley Mangrum came looking for his boy. Jimmy had about given up hope that his daddy cared anything about him when, least expected, one evening there he was. Jimmy and I were sitting on the front porch after dinner annoying the old man's cat with a piece of broom straw. The old man was sprawled on his glider and, like the cat, was trying to relax his way into a good night's sleep.

"You boys leave that cat alone and go clean up the kitchen."

Even as he spoke, a 1983 Ford pickup with a camper shell pulled into the gravel driveway and rolled up to the house. It was Jimmy's daddy. He got out of the pickup and walked up to the porch.

"I come for my boy," he said, speaking directly to the old man. Almost as an afterthought he turned toward Jimmy. "Hello, son," he said.

The old man didn't say a word, just stared at him. When he finally spoke it was to Jimmy. "Go and get your things. Your daddy's come to take you home." That said, he got up and walked into the house, followed closely by Jimmy. I was left sitting on the porch.

Turley's face flushed red. "I guess your old grandpap don't much approve of me," he said.

I shrugged.

"Well, anyhow, don't think I don't appreciate what you

two done, taking him in and all." He paused and lit a cigarette. "If that don't beat all," he continued, "his momma just leaving him like that. Boy," he said, pointing his cigarette at me, "let that be a lesson to you."

"Yessir," I said.

I drove out to see Jimmy the next day. The house his daddy had rented was a miserable little frame box set up on cinder blocks. It looked like a strong wind might blow it over. Inside there were just three rooms: living room, kitchen, and bedroom. Jimmy and his daddy both seemed pleased to see me.

"Hey, bo'," his daddy said, "come on in and have a beer."

We walked through the small living room into the kitchen. Dirty dishes from several meals were piled on the table and in the sink.

"Don't worry about the mess," Turley said.

We all grabbed a beer out of the icebox and trooped back into the living room. Jimmy and I sat on the only piece of furniture in the room, a ratty-looking sofa. His daddy stood by the door and drained his can of beer in one long swallow.

"You boys rest easy for a spell. I got some business to tend to."

He left the house and drove away in his truck. I turned to Jimmy.

"Where's his girlfriend?"

Jimmy cut his eyes toward the closed door to the bedroom.

"She's in there." He lowered his voice. "She and Daddy were going at it hot and heavy this morning."

I leaned in, interested. "No shit."

He giggled. "Sounded like a couple of hogs rootin' around."

Before we could say more, the bedroom door opened, and a young girl walked out. She looked at the two of us.

"Where's your daddy gone?" she asked Jimmy.

"He didn't say. Said he'd be back directly." Jimmy pointed at me. "This here's my friend Pete."

I nodded at her. Although only a couple of years older than me and Jimmy she looked aged, like maybe Charleston hadn't agreed with her.

"Howdy, ma'am." I wasn't sure what to say.

If looks could have killed I'd have been dead on the floor.

"I ain't no 'ma'am'," she said and walked back into the bedroom, closing the door behind her.

Jimmy looked at me and made a back and forth motion with his forearm, his fist clenched. We both laughed.

Turley Mangrum seemed to be everything a boy could want in a father. A veteran of a two-year hitch in the army (a good deal of which, he proudly told us, he spent in the stockade), he had what Jimmy and I thought of as a wonderfully romantic past. In addition to the army he had been a carnival roustabout, a rod-and-chain man on a state surveying crew, and a driver for several distillers and distributors of illegal whiskey in eastern North Carolina. He smoked Luckies, liked to keep a fresh toothpick in the corner of his mouth at all times, and had a tattoo of an eagle with the words *Death Before Dishonor* on his left biceps.

"Now, you boys can't be calling me 'Daddy' or 'Sir' when we're out chasing women."

Turley got two phony ID cards for Jimmy and me and began taking us to his favorite roadhouse over in Wake County. He insisted we both call him Turley and promised to get us laid at the first opportunity. Being married as well as having a girlfriend with a baby seemed to be of no particular inconvenience to him, for he slept with most any woman that would go to bed with him. The three of us spent more and more time together, staying out most of the night and sleeping the better part of the day.

By the time July had thinned out pretty near to August the old man made his move.

"Boy," he told me, "I'm going to tell you straight out. Turley Mangrum is nothing but trash, pure and simple. Do you get my point?"

I knew what he had in mind. The hard part was telling Jimmy that I couldn't hang out with him and his daddy anymore. Although Jimmy seemed hurt and angry, his daddy tried to smooth things over.

"Don't you worry about a thing," he told me. "Jimmy and me'll do just fine. You listen at what your old grandpap tells you. He don't mean nothing bad by it, that's just the way old folks are."

Of course I still saw them both at ballgames and such. Jimmy and I played American Legion ball that summer, and Turley generally came to all the games. We'd stand around and drink a beer afterwards, and they'd tell me what they'd been up to. Jimmy bragged about how he and his daddy both had gotten a dose of the clap from a mill worker over in Durham. They laughed when they saw my wide eyes and open mouth.

"Shoot," Turley said, nudging Jimmy with his elbow, "you ain't a man until you've had your first dose. It's no worse than a bad cold."

Towards the end of August Turley's girlfriend left him and moved back in with her folks in Fuquay-Varina, taking the baby with her. After the last game of the season, in Zebulon, Turley, Jimmy, and I were leaning against Turley's Ford chewing Red Man tobacco and spitting at ants. The summer had wound down like an old pocketwatch put away in a dresser drawer and forgotten. I casually mentioned that school would be starting soon. Our senior year. Jimmy gave me a flat-eyed, expressionless look.

"I ain't planning on going back to high school."

I was stunned. "What are you going to do?"

"I don't rightly know yet."

"Well, what will your momma say?"

Jimmy lit a cigarette and shifted the toothpick he had started keeping in the corner of his mouth. He winked at his daddy. "Fuck her," he said.

Right after the first of September, with just a week or so left before school started, Jimmy told me that he had joined the marines and would be leaving for Parris Island in ten days. I didn't know what to say. We had always talked about joining the army together after graduation, but of course his decision to quit school had queered that. I guess I had hoped that when push came to shove he would change his mind and come back and finish high school with me.

"Well, goddamn, Jimmy. Congratulations. I'll be damned. The marines." I pumped his hand, not knowing what to say, feeling just awful about it.

"Yeah, I had me enough of this bullshit. Figured I better get a head start on you and see some of the world."

Although his words were bold he seemed unsettled, unsure about what he had done. It was as if he felt guilty about it, sneaking off as it were, letting me down somehow. We stood there for a moment, not speaking, suddenly uncomfortable in each other's presence.

"Hey." Jimmy broke the awkward silence. "Listen. Me and Turley are throwing a big party next Saturday. Why don't you come on over. It's my last Saturday night as a civilian."

I said something like "Hey, you bet," but I think we both knew that I wouldn't be dropping by. I never saw him again.

I graduated in May and sort of half expected to see Jimmy at the graduation ceremony, but of course he never showed up. Back when we were in the tenth grade Jimmy and I had started talking about Virginia Beach. We swore that when we graduated we would go up there for at least a week, maybe two, and do nothing but lay on the sand and drink beer. It was no big deal, just the sort of foolish thing kids will talk about for years and then end up never doing. Still, I found myself looking around for him at graduation, wondering if he remembered.

And the darnedest thing of all. That winter, four or five months after Jimmy went into the marines, his daddy, Turley, killed himself with a .44 magnum pistol. Jimmy never even showed up at the funeral. Have you got words?

Blackstone

Blackstone, Virginia, suffered the summer heat like a fat man at a Pentecostal revival: writhing and shifting uncomfortably on an unforgiving pine bench, soaked with the stale sweat of confession. Little of value graced Blackstone's dry and barren fields. The town was so poor it had no stone memorial honoring its Confederate war dead.

"I'd like to rent a cabin."

She was tired, bone weary, and looked it. It was mid-morning, August 1956, and she had driven all night from Detroit, fighting high beams and drowsiness with only an old man and a boy for company.

"One cabin for the three of you?"

Vernon Gates was the sole proprietor of the Blackstone Tourist Court. He was sixty-three years old and, except for three years in Petersburg when he was married, had lived in

Blackstone all his life. Vernon built the Tourist Court in 1942 and prospered almost immediately, renting cabins and selling whiskey to the soldiers stationed at nearby Camp Pickett. When the war ended, Camp Pickett closed, and the dust of hard times settled once again over the county.

"No," the woman answered, "just for me and the boy. I'll be taking Daddy out to the Baptist Home as soon as we get unpacked."

("Are we Baptists, Momma?" the boy had asked from the back seat, somewhere south of Wheeling, West Virginia.)

"Cabins are twenty dollars a week." Mr. Gates cleared his throat. "In advance." When she gave him the money, he pulled a large key from his pocket and handed it to her. "Take number 4. Not much for a boy to do around here."

The cabin, fourth in a row of twelve, sat baking in the sunlight like a particularly ugly cake, viscous drops of tar oozing from beneath the corrugated tin roof. They unloaded their luggage—a cardboard-sided grip tied up with cotton twine and a Piggly Wiggly bag stuffed with underwear and socks. Without stopping to unpack, the woman left to take her father out to the Home. The boy, ordered to nap until she returned, got out of bed as soon as his mother was gone. He wandered around the one large room, examining every detail of every object. On one wall, next to the bathroom door, was a white porcelain sink and a mirror. The sink was chipped and badly stained, and the mirror had a large crack running diagonally across its face. Someone had tried to repair the crack by covering it with several strips of cellophane tape, which had fused and yellowed in the heat and humidity of central Virginia. By standing on the wastebasket and hold-ing his head just so, the boy found he could create a split image of himself in the mirror, an image he found amusing for quite some time.

Finally bored with the contents and furnishings of the cabin, he opened the screen door and stepped outside. He wandered slowly up to the cabin that served as both home and office to Vernon Gates, attracted by the bright red Coca-Cola chest he had seen on the covered porch when they ar-rived. A voice from the shadows at the end of the porch startled him.

"I reckon your momma told you not to get into any trou-ble, didn't she?" The voice belonged to Mr. Gates.

"Yessir." The boy stood in the sun, staring down at his scuffed tennis shoes.

"Told her there weren't much around here for a boy to do." Vernon saw Danny glancing at the Coke chest. "I expect you'd like a Dr. Pepper or a Nehi one."

"Yessir."

"Look at me when you talk, boy. Ain't nothing worse than a man who won't look you in the eye when he talks to you. You got any money?"

"No sir."

Vernon grunted. "I didn't think so. Well, come on up here and get yourself one anyway. You can pay me later."

Danny jumped up on the porch and opened the chest. In-side, sitting in cool water four inches deep, were tens of bot-tles of soft drinks: Cokes, Pepsis, Nehis, Dr. Peppers, and RC Colas. It was a wonderful sight. The sweet, orangy taste of the Nehi he selected was so good it made him shiver in the hot air.

"How old are you, boy?"

"Eight." He was only seven but thought it prudent to add a year when talking to strangers, particularly since he was small for his age.

"What's your name?"

"Danny."

"Where's your pa?"

Danny shook his head, his attention focused on his orange soda.

"You don't know or your ma told you not to say?"

"Don't know." Danny finished the Nehi and put the empty bottle into a wooden crate sitting next to the chest. He did so regretfully, sorry that the drink was gone so quickly. He could think of no luxury greater than to be able to buy two sodas at once so you could drink the first one as fast as you wanted, knowing that the second one remained to be lingered over and savored. He looked at Mr. Gates. "Thank you for the Nehi."

Vernon nodded. "Well, your momma taught you some manners, I can see that. Ain't nothing worse than a boy without manners." Vernon suddenly thought of something the boy might be interested in. "The county reservoir is only about three-quarters of a mile from here. You and your mother might enjoy going over for a swim one of these afternoons. They've got a big raft anchored out in the middle that all the kids like to swim out to."

Danny nodded politely but said nothing, experience telling him his mother would enjoy no such thing.

"You better get along over to your cabin now, before she comes back."

Inside the cabin again Danny bounced up and down on the bed until his mother returned.

"Here," she said, placing a paper sack on top of the dresser. "I brought you some dinner."

"What is it?" Danny asked.

"Brunswick stew and hush puppies. Come on now, get off that bed before this stuff gets cold."

"Aren't you going to eat anything?" he asked, nibbling on a hush puppy.

"I ate a bite while they was putting this up." She poured some of the thick stew out of its thin cardboard container onto a paper plate and handed it to the boy.

Danny sat on the bed and began to eat. "Is Grandpa going to die?" he asked.

His mother lit a cigarette and walked into the tiny bathroom. She didn't answer.

"Just passing through?" Vernon held the cabin key in his right hand, not quite willing to hand it over.

"Hard to say. I might just decide to set a spell."

He was a young man, no more than twenty-two or twenty-three from the look of things.

"What's your name?"

"Murdoch, Billy Murdoch."

"You're not from around here." It was more a statement than a question.

Billy Murdoch smiled, and Vernon suddenly wanted not to rent him a cabin.

"My people come from over near Newport News," Billy said vaguely.

"What is it that you do?" the old man asked.

Billy took out a pack of Camels and offered one to the old man. "Smoke?" When Mr. Gates declined, he carefully placed one between his lips and lit it with a kitchen match he took from his other pocket. "Bibles."

"Bibles? You sell Bibles?"

Billy exhaled a long stream of cigarette smoke, ending his exhalation with a perfectly blown smoke ring. He carefully examined the burnt match as if written on it he would find the answer to something he had puzzled over for quite some time. "That's right." His eyes raised from the now-cold match and seized the old man. "Do you read the Scriptures?"

Vernon Gates snorted, his sudden fear of the soft-spoken young man in front of him gone. "The cabin's four dollars a night or twenty dollars a week. In advance."

Billy threw a twenty-dollar bill on the counter. "Who belongs to the Ford?" he asked, cutting his eyes past the old man to the dusty automobile sitting in front of cabin number 4.

"That'll be Miz Parker." Vernon handed Billy the cabin key. "She and her boy are stayin' here whilst she gets her father situated in the Baptist Home outside town."

"She got no man with her?"

The way he asked, the slow, measured beat of his words

as he spoke, troubled Vernon, and he once again began to doubt.

"That's none of my business," he said, wanting to say *that's none of* your *business,* but holding off.

Billy laughed, a short, two-bark sound, and walked out of the office. He got into his car, a 1955 Mercury, and wheeled into the unpaved courtyard. He parked directly in front of the Ford and got out and walked back to the rear of his car, standing quietly for several seconds before opening his trunk and taking out a single suitcase. He fumbled in his pocket for the key Mr. Gates had given him and dropped it into the dust between the two automobiles. He took something else from his pocket and quickly knelt down, ostensibly to retrieve the dropped key. Shielded from the door to cabin number 4 by the front of the Ford, he reached his right hand into the Ford's right front wheel well. A quiet but steady hiss of escaping air came from the tire as he withdrew his hand and picked up the cabin key, standing up in one smooth motion. Smiling, he reached down for the suitcase and walked casually to his cabin.

"Ma'am?"

It was just past five o'clock in the afternoon, and although the sun had begun its slow decline toward evening there was no noticeable relief from the fierce heat that gripped the Blackstone Tourist Court.

"Ma'am?"

Billy Murdoch knocked again at the screen door to cabin number 4. Danny's mother came to the door and peered out through the dusty screen. She was barefoot and wore a light cotton shift of indeterminate color. Her Tonied curls sprang out wildly in the heat and humidity. Behind her, on the bed, Danny lay sleeping, curled into a fetal position, thumb in mouth. She didn't say anything, just looked out at Billy.

"I'm sorry to disturb you, ma'am, I surely am, but I'm afraid you've gone and got yourself a flat tire."

"What?"

"Yes, ma'am." Billy nodded, his face clouded with neighborly concern and great regret. "I checked in about an hour ago and just this minute noticed that you've got a flat tire. I thought you should know about it if you didn't already." He smiled suddenly. "My name's Billy Murdoch."

The smile, seemingly so spontaneous, confused the young woman, and she instinctively raised a hand to her hair. "Ruth Ann," she said, pushing at the unruly results of her home perm. "Ruth Ann Parker." She pushed the door open and stepped out into the sunlight.

"It's on the other side," Billy said helpfully, walking around the front end of her car and pointing to the right front tire. He smiled again. "I'll be happy to change it for you."

"Damn." Ruth Ann shook her head. "I don't have a spare." She looked at Billy. "What'll I do?"

Danny woke up slowly, the stifling heat in the cabin dulling his senses. There was radio music coming from one of the other cabins and periodically the laughter of a man and a woman. After a time he realized that it was evening and that the cabin in which he lay drowsing was dark, as was the courtyard beyond the screen door. He got off the bed and walked out into the courtyard, drawn by the sounds of country music and his mother's voice. He stopped outside the door to cabin number 6, bathed in the wan yellow light coming through the torn screen. His mother was sitting on the bed kissing a strange man whose hands were touching her in places he never saw anyone touch before. Next to the bed, on the nightstand, sat an empty pint bottle of whiskey and two glasses. After what seemed like the longest time the two of them sensed that someone was watching through the door, and the man stood up from the bed with a curse. Danny stumbled back a step and turned and ran back to his own cabin, his mother in close pursuit. Inside their cabin she angrily grabbed his arm and put her face down next to his.

"What were you doing snooping around like that?" she demanded, her breath heavy with alcohol. "If I catch you spying on me I swear I'll wear you out, you hear me?" For emphasis she gave him a good shake, rattling his head back and forth.

"Oh, hell, let the boy be."

Billy Murdoch stood in the cabin's door, leaning casually against the jamb. "He was probably just hungry." Billy winked at the thoroughly frightened Danny. "God knows, I sure as hell am." He inclined his head out toward his Mercury parked in the courtyard. "Let's go get us a bite to eat."

After dinner Ruth Ann and Billy dropped Danny off at the Tourist Court.

"You go on in and get ready for bed," Ruth Ann told him. "I'll be back directly after me and Billy take us a little drive."

Danny stood at the screen door and watched Billy Murdoch's Mercury pull out onto the road. Instead of going in as his mother had told him he stood outside in the dark, watching the lightning bugs darting among the cabins. He saw the glow of a cigarette on the porch of Mr. Gates's cabin and walked over.

"I see you're back from dinner," Vernon said.

"Yessir." Danny sat down on the edge of the porch. He knew where the Coca-Cola chest should be, sitting against the wall, but could not quite make it out. "Why are you sitting in the dark?" he asked.

"I don't much crave the company of insects," came the languid reply. "Too, if I had a light on people could see me sitting here."

"Why don't you want anyone to see you?" Danny asked.

"Because a man should be able to relax in the evening without worrying about folks seein' him. You know what I'm talking about?"

Danny shook his head. "No sir," he said.

Vernon pinched out his cigarette and put the butt in his shirt pocket. "You will when you're older. Where's your momma?" Vernon had seen her drive off with Billy Murdoch but was curious as to what the boy would say.

"She and Billy went for a drive," Danny replied. "We had dinner at the Little Acorn," he added.

"You call him Billy instead of Mr. Murdoch?"

Danny was suddenly defensive. "He told me to," he said quickly. "Said his pa was Mr. Murdoch."

Vernon snorted. "Is that a fact? What'd you eat over at the Acorn?"

"I had barbecue and slaw," Danny said, happy for the change in subject. "Momma and..." he glanced quickly in Mr. Gates's direction, "...and Billy had the fried chicken."

The old man and the boy sat quietly then on the porch, neither able to think of anything further to talk about.

Vernon shifted in his chair. "You better run along back to your cabin now and get into bed before your momma gets home," he told Danny.

Danny got up at once. "Yessir," he said and quickly disappeared into the darkness.

Vernon relit his cigarette and sat in the dark, alone once again, absentmindedly rubbing his crotch with his right hand as he thought about Billy Murdoch and the boy's mother. Later, in bed, he awoke briefly when the two of them drove in. He fumbled with the old Elgin on the nightstand, using the sliver of moonlight falling across his bed to illuminate the dial. It was 3 A.M.

At eight the next morning Danny got up quietly, careful not to wake his mother. He walked outside and saw Mr. Gates sitting on his porch fanning himself.

"You had any breakfast yet?"

Danny shook his head. "Momma's still sleeping," he said. He pointed to the fan Mr. Gates was holding. It was made out of woven coconut palm strips. "What's that?"

"That's a fan, boy," Vernon replied, mild exasperation evident in his voice. "Given out by the ladies of the Calvary Free Will Baptist Church." He held it out to Danny. "Would you like to have it?"

Danny took the fan and examined it. "I never seen one like this before. What's these leaves from?"

"Them's palm leaves. The ladies give the fans out for Palm Sunday," Vernon said.

"What's Palm Sunday?"

"Hell, boy, ain't you never been to Sunday School?"

Danny looked down at his tennis shoes. "If you give me your fan, won't you get hot?"

"It's kind of you to be so considerate," Vernon said, "but as it happens I got more fans than Carter's got pills. All the churches, cemeteries, and funeral homes hereabouts give them away. The business of being borned again and dying is a powerful hot one." Vernon could see that the boy hadn't the faintest idea what he was talking about. "I asked you if you'd had any breakfast."

Danny shook his head. "No sir," he said.

Vernon pushed himself out of his rocker. "Well," he said, "I was just fixin' to make myself a cup of coffee and some toast. Would you like some?"

"Momma won't let me have any coffee," Danny said.

Vernon looked annoyed. "Damn it, boy, your momma's not here. Do you want a cup of coffee and some toast or not?"

Danny drew back, unsure of why Mr. Gates was suddenly short with him. "No sir," he said, "Momma'd be mad. Thank you for the fan." He walked quickly back to his cabin and sat quietly fanning himself until his mother woke up.

"Can I come with you to see Grandpa today?" Danny sat on the edge of the bed and watched his mother put on her lipstick. She had to keep bobbing her head back and forth to get an image undistorted by the crack in the mirror.

"I'm not going out to the Home today," she said.

Danny smiled, suddenly excited. "Are we going swimming today?" At dinner the evening before, Danny had told his mother and Billy Murdoch about the county reservoir, and Billy had promptly promised to take the boy swimming.

"This damned humidity has done ruined my hair," she muttered. She finally turned from the mirror and looked at Danny. "What did you say?"

"I asked if you was going to come swimming with me and Billy today," Danny said.

"No," she said, "I'm driving with Billy over to Petersburg in a little bit. You're going to have to look after yourself today. Here…," she handed him a dollar bill from her purse, "this is for your lunch. And mind I want the change back."

"Can't I go with you to Petersburg?" He had no idea where or even what Petersburg was but he badly wanted not to be left behind.

"No," his mother replied, "we're going over with another couple. Grownups. You get you some lunch and then go on down to that lake or reservoir or something. We'll most likely be back before dark." She paused for a moment. "Maybe we'll get some ice cream after dinner."

The reservoir was deserted when Danny arrived, and the lack of other swimmers made him feel the absence of any friends of his own even more strongly. A large wooden raft, the one Mr. Gates had spoken of, was anchored some fifty yards offshore. Danny shielded his eyes with his left hand, Indian-style, and squinted into the distance. The raft appeared to be many miles away. He played on the shore, skipping stones across the lake, until a group of teenagers arrived. He watched from a distance as the three boys and two girls plunged in and swam out to the raft. Emboldened, he walked into the water. Unsure of himself once he got in, he stayed close to the shore, in water no more than waist-deep, while he practiced flailing his arms and kicking his legs. With no encouragement he rapidly tired and lost interest.

"Whatcha been up to all day?"

Danny stood on Mr. Gates's porch, a cool Nehi orange in his hand. He had returned from the lake three hours earlier and stayed in his cabin until he saw the old man come out onto his porch. He solemnly handed Mr. Gates a dime and shrugged in response to the question.

"Nothin'." Danny opened his drink and looked at Mr. Gates. "You weren't out on your porch all afternoon." It was more an accusation than a question. The old man laughed.

"Well, sir," he said, "this heat has done given me a case of the fantods, so naturally I took to my bed to sweat 'em out."

"What's the fantods?" Danny asked.

"It's something old folks get from time to time. Makes

'em mean and ornery. Nothing for a young fellow like you to worry about."

"Will my grandpa get the fantods?" Danny persisted.

"Most likely," Mr. Gates answered. He flipped the dime the boy had given him into the air, caught it, and handed it back. "Keep it," he said. "You and your friend Billy go swimming today?"

Danny carefully sighted over the top of the Nehi bottle, looking down toward his cabin. "Billy and Momma went off to Petersburg," he said. "I went down to the lake by myself." He finished the orange drink and sighed.

"Something the matter?" Vernon Gates asked.

"No sir," Danny answered as he stepped off the porch.

Vernon frowned but didn't say anything as he watched the boy walk back to his cabin.

In the cabin Danny sat on the bed methodically punching one of the feather pillows. He stayed awake as long as he could after evening enveloped the Tourist Court but finally fell asleep, fully clothed, just before midnight. Dawn was decidedly more than just a hint in the eastern sky when his mother returned. Danny barely stirred when she lay down on the bed next to him.

"Who taught you how to swim?"

Danny and Vernon Gates were cutting through the field behind the Blackstone Tourist Court on their way to the county reservoir. It was just eleven o'clock in the morning, and already the sun seemed to be suspended no more than seventy-five or a hundred yards above the parched Virginia countryside. Danny's mother had risen quite unsteadily that morning and after emerging from the bathroom, where she had vomited several times, had made it quite clear that Danny's presence in the small cabin would not be particularly appreciated.

"No one."

Danny had seen Mr. Gates sitting out on his covered porch and had walked down, uninvited, to sit with him.

"What's your ma up to this morning?"

Danny shook his head, wanting to ask for a Nehi soda but knowing instinctively not to. "She's sick."

"Is that a fact?" Vernon had heard Ruth Ann and Billy Murdoch drive into the courtyard at dawn that morning. He figured that what ailed the boy's mother had more to do with distilled spirits than any virus that might be going around. Still, he'd been drunk a time or two himself when he was her age. "Have you et anything yet this morning?"

"No sir." Danny hoped the old man might offer him a soda.

"Are you hungry?"

Danny shrugged.

With a sigh, Vernon pushed himself up from his rocker. "Come on in and I'll see what's in the icebox."

While his host scrambled eggs and toasted bread Danny looked around the small living area of Mr. Gates's rustic cabin. He spotted a photograph of a young woman dressed in old-fashioned clothes and carried it into the kitchen. "Who is this?" he asked.

"My wife."

"Is she dead?"

Vernon chuckled, pleased at the boy's naive forthright-ness. "Deader 'n a doornail," he answered, for it was true.

Danny nodded gravely. "I think my grandpa's going to die soon," he said, hoping it would make Mr. Gates feel better to hear it.

"Do tell." Vernon spread the eggs onto two plates. "I wouldn't be in any big rush to go burying him just yet if I was you. Old folks'll fool you sometimes when it comes to dying, don't you know. Let's eat."

After they had eaten and Vernon had drunk a cup of coffee and smoked a cigarette, the boy suggested that they might want to go swimming. Vernon took an exaggerated look at the sun and shook his head.

"It's too hot, boy. That sun'll plumb fry us out there."

Danny's shoulders sagged, and the old man sighed.

"All right, all right, go and get your bathing trunks on and tell your ma where you're going. I expect she'll want to know."

Danny ran to his cabin, excited that Mr. Gates had agreed to walk down to the reservoir with him. He hesitated at the screen door, his enthusiasm tempered by the recollection of his mother's foul mood that morning. He decided that if she were asleep he would change into his bathing suit and leave without waking her. Although it was relatively dark in the cabin he saw that she was still lying down, facing away from him with a sheet lightly covering her, and someone was sit-ting on the bed next to her. It was Billy Murdoch.

"Hey, kid," Billy asked, not unkindly, "whatcha up to this morning?"

Danny looked uncertainly from his mother, still lying with her back to him, to Billy, who was smoking a cigarette and resting his other hand casually on Ruth Ann's hip.

"Swimmin'," Danny answered, his voice barely audible.

"Swimming? That sounds like a hell of an idea." Billy turned his head and slapped Ruth Ann lightly on the buttocks. "What do you say we go down to the swimming hole with the kid here?"

Ruth Ann lay still for a moment, not answering, and then quickly got up from the bed, totally unclothed, and brushed past Danny on her way to the bathroom. She slammed the door behind her. The two of them, Danny and Billy, presently heard her struggling with the dry heaves. Billy laughed and pointed his cigarette at the boy.

"I've never knowed a woman yet could hold her liquor," Billy said, as if passing on a profound piece of knowledge to the boy. He shook his head while saying it, as if unable to imagine such an astounding thing, but knowing it to be true nonetheless. "You let that be a lesson to you, boy," he added cryptically.

Danny, shaken by his mother's nakedness as well as the sound of her efforts to throw up, said nothing. He hurried into his trunks, anxious to be away from Billy Murdoch.

The old man and the boy stood on a bank overlooking the county reservoir. Vernon Gates wore a large Panama straw hat to protect himself from the sun. He pointed his finger across the water, out to where the raft floated benignly.

"Can you swim out that far?"

Danny shrugged his shoulders and then quickly shook his head. He couldn't even imagine it.

"Billy said he'd teach me, though. Said he'd teach me how to swim."

"I thought you told me you already could swim."

"Not for-real swimming." Danny looked down at his dusty tennis shoes. "Not out to there." He looked up at the old man. "Can you swim? Out to the raft?"

Before Vernon could answer, a voice called out from behind them. They both turned around and saw Billy Murdoch striding across the fallow field they had just crossed. He quickly caught up to where they stood.

"Thought I'd join you for a little swim." Billy grinned and winked at Mr. Gates. He nodded back in the general direction of the Tourist Court. "Man can't be riding no sick mule."

Vernon flushed, angered that Billy would speak even obliquely in such a manner about Ruth Ann while the boy was in earshot. Billy, oblivious to Vernon's disapproval, put his hand on Danny's shoulder.

"Come on, kid, I'll give you that swimming lesson I promised you."

Billy dropped his trousers, revealing a pair of khaki shorts, and kicked off his brogans. He picked his way gingerly across the reservoir's narrow, rocky beach, the soles of his feet obviously shoe-soft. His body was white and whipcord hard, and he dove without hesitation into the reservoir, disappearing beneath the glassy water only to surface ten feet or more out from the shore. The sunlight glared off the wetness on his back, and Danny had to squint to see him. He swam effortlessly, his head turning rhythmically from one side to the other, and in a wondrously short time he was climbing the ladder onto the raft. He waved at Danny and Vernon, and then dove back into the water. At the shore, he walked out to rejoin them, water running off the tight skin of his body in quicksilver rivulets that gathered here and there and were gone too quickly to follow. Danny could clearly see the outline of Billy's penis through the thin, khaki shorts, and he looked away, embarrassed.

"Now," Billy said, wiping the water from his face, "the thing about swimming is, you just get in and do it." He looked down at Danny. "You understand what I'm telling you?"

Danny looked up at Billy, his eyes wide. He shook his head, certain that Billy wasn't telling him what he needed to know. Billy, for his part, having expected Danny to just jump in and start paddling, wasn't sure what to do next. He decided another demonstration was needed.

"Watch me," he said, "and do like I do."

Behind Danny, and unseen by him, Vernon shook his head with disgust and turned to walk back to the cabins.

Billy eased into the water and swam back and forth parallel to the shore. "Like that," he called out to the boy, "just like that." He swam another lap for emphasis and then waded ashore. "There," he said, quite pleased with himself, "now do you understand?"

Danny knew that he was still missing something but was afraid to say so. He nodded affirmatively.

Billy was satisfied. "Good," he said. "You just practice for a while, and I expect that in a day or two you'll be ready to swim out to the raft with me, won't you?"

"Yessir," Danny said. He walked into the warm water and began splashing about. Only after several minutes had passed did he realize that Mr. Gates was nowhere to be seen. Billy, sunbathing on the shore, saw the boy looking about and laughed.

"If you're looking for that old man, he's done gone. My advice would be to forget about him. An old fool like that's never going to do you any good, if you get my point." Billy paused for a moment. "I believe I'll ease on back and see how your momma's feeling. Why don't you stick around here for a while?"

Before Danny could answer, Billy was gone, his trousers thrown over one shoulder as he hurried across the field, anxious to be out of the hot sun. Danny turned back to the shore and imagined himself cleaving fearlessly through the water, a group of admiring young people urging him on. He sat down on a large rock and waited as long as he could, knowing that his mother didn't want him hanging around the cabin. Finally, unable to stay alone at the reservoir any longer, he walked slowly back.

Billy and Ruth Ann were getting into the Mercury just as Danny strolled slowly into the Tourist Court's courtyard.

"We're going to get us a touch of the hair of the dog that bit us last night, kid," Billy said. Danny's mother was wearing a kerchief over her hair and had on a pair of sunglasses he had not seen before. Billy winked at the boy. "Too bad you're not a little older or you could come along."

"Hush," Ruth Ann said to Billy. She turned to Danny. "We should be back before dinner. I fixed a cheese sandwich for your lunch and left it on the bureau." She handed Danny a dime out the car window. "Get you a soda to have with it."

Billy started the Mercury and revved the engine, grinning at the reverberating roar from the fiberglass-packed mufflers. Ruth Ann grimaced and held her hands over her ears, and Danny involuntarily backed two steps away from the side of the car. After they left Danny walked into the cabin and threw the cheese sandwich into the toilet.

"What's a 'hair of the dog'?"

Vernon looked at the boy carefully. It was just past six in the evening, and the two of them were sitting on Mr. Gates's porch. "Where did you hear that particular expression?"

"Billy said that's what he and Momma were going to get."

Vernon smiled for the boy's benefit. "Well, that's just a way of saying they were going to get something to make her feel a little better. Didn't you tell me she was feeling right poorly this morning?"

Danny nodded. "It's something you get from the drugstore?"

"Sometimes."

"Sounds funny." Danny yawned and then sighed. "How come you left me and Billy at the reservoir this morning?"

Vernon didn't say anything for the longest time. "Are you hungry?" he finally asked.

"Yessir."

Dinner was a simple affair, a warmed-up can of beans into which several hot dogs had been cut up, the whole concoction dosed liberally with ketchup and served with white bread on the side. Danny watched Mr. Gates eat by troweling the beans from his plate onto a piece of bread and he imitated everything the old man did, down to hunching his back and keeping both of his forearms on the table on either side of his plate. Vernon noticed and at once sat up straight in his chair.

"Here, now," he said, pointing his fork at the boy, "don't be leaning over your food like that. And keep your arms off the table."

Confused, Danny did as he was told.

"I been eating alone for so long that I forget my table manners," Vernon said, "so don't you be studying the way I do things." He chuckled as he wiped his plate clean with a last piece of bread. "You eat that way around your mother and we'll both be in trouble."

After dinner the two of them retired once again to the porch.

"You mind when you first came here I asked you about your pa?"

Danny sat with his knees drawn up to his chest. He nodded in response to Mr. Gates's question.

"Did you ever know him?"

Danny shook his head.

"Does your mother ever talk about him?"

Again Danny shook his head. Before either of them could say anything further Billy Murdoch's Mercury swerved into the courtyard from the county blacktop road, tires squealing, narrowly missing the corner of the first cabin. Billy and Ruth Ann were in the front seat and another couple sat in the rear. Danny jumped from the porch and ran to the Mercury as Billy parked it in front of Ruth Ann's Ford.

"I'll just be a minute," Ruth Ann said to Billy as she got out of the car carrying a paper sack. Her face was flushed and she stumbled slightly as she walked into the cabin.

Billy sat behind the Mercury's steering wheel, a Dixie cup in his right hand and his left arm hanging out the window. "Hey, kid," he said to Danny as the boy walked past the car, following his mother into the cabin. His lips were wet and soft-looking, and he frightened Danny.

In the cabin Ruth Ann took two small cardboard containers out of the bag she had brought from the car. "Come here," she said, motioning to Danny. "I brought you some dinner."

"I ate with Mr. Gates," Danny said proudly, thinking she would be pleased. "He invited me."

"Goddamn it," Ruth Ann cursed, suddenly angry. "I go to all the trouble to come back here to bring you some dinner and you tell me you've already eaten." Her right hand flashed out and struck Danny on the side of his face, knocking him against the bed. The blow startled Ruth Ann as much as the boy. She hurried from the cabin and rejoined Billy Murdoch and the other couple in the Mercury. Billy started the car and roared out of the courtyard.

Vernon Gates, unaware of what had transpired between Danny and Ruth Ann, remained on his porch, smoking a cigarette. It was a pleasant evening, with a lingering rose color in the sky that promised another clear, hot day on the morrow. Just at full dark Vernon heard, rather than saw, the screen door on Ruth Ann's cabin open and shut, and he smiled, knowing that the boy would soon be on his steps.

"I expect you'll be wanting a Nehi soda," he said as Danny sat down.

Danny shook his head and sniffled.

"What's the matter?" the old man asked, suddenly concerned. He reached up and turned on the porch light and was shocked at what he saw. He quickly turned the light off. "That's quite a shiner you're developing," he said, his voice soft. "Did your ma do that to you?"

Danny nodded but did not speak.

"Do you know why?"

Danny's voice was barely audible. "She was mad because I ate dinner with you."

Vernon nodded although of course the boy could not see him in the dark. "I think maybe you should go to bed now," he finally said. "I'll have a little talk with your ma in the morning and tell her it was my doing that you had dinner with me tonight."

Vernon sat quietly on his porch for some time, watching the lightning bugs dance in the courtyard. Finally he got up and went inside to use the telephone.

When Danny woke up he knew it was early, because the courtyard through the screen door was bathed in a pearl-colored light, and had a softness about it that the harsh summer sun would soon dispel. He heard the faint buzz of voices coming from the direction of Mr. Gates's residence, and he rose from the bed, taking care not to disturb his mother. He pushed open the screen door and saw Mr. Gates talking to two men and pointing toward Billy Murdoch's cabin. The men wore tight fitting khaki shirts and Sam Browne belts and Danny knew immediately that they were policemen. Their car, a late-model Ford with a large, red light on its roof, sat at the entrance to the courtyard. Suddenly fearful, he quickly stepped back into the cabin and peered out from behind the screen door. The policemen walked up to Billy's cabin and, without bothering to knock, opened the screen door and went inside. Scarcely breathing, Danny stood watching, his eyes wide.

"What is it?" Ruth Ann, propped up on one elbow, spoke to Danny from the bed. "What are you looking at?"

"It's the police," Danny answered. "They've gone into Billy's cabin."

Ruth Ann quickly rose and went to the door, taking care to stand well back in the shadows that filled the room. She took both of Danny's arms in her hands and held him tightly. After the longest time the policemen emerged from the cabin, Billy Murdoch in handcuffs between them. He was barefoot and wore only his trousers. They walked him across the courtyard to their car and carefully put him into the back seat. Mr. Gates, his arms folded across his chest, stood watching from his porch.

"I appreciate the phone call, Vernon," the older policeman said after Billy was put into the car. "You were sure enough right about something being queer about him. He admitted right off he was AWOL from the army over at Fort Lee. Said he stole the car in Richmond last week."

Vernon Gates nodded but said nothing.

"Now, what about the woman and boy? You want us to check her out?"

Vernon shook his head. "I expect everything will settle down now that you've got that trash," he nodded toward Billy, slumped in the back seat of the police car, "locked up."

"Good enough. I'll have someone out to pick up the car later this morning. You call me if something comes up with the woman."

They drove off, and in a second all that was left of Billy Murdoch was the dust settling slowly back down onto the courtyard. Vernon sat down and lit a cigarette. When he had smoked it he went inside to fix his breakfast.

"We're leaving."

Vernon looked at Ruth Ann, saw the harsh set of her mouth, and nodded his head.

"Here."

She handed him the key to the cabin and turned immediately from the porch. In the car, Danny sat looking straight ahead as his mother drove from the courtyard. Vernon, feeling suddenly fatigued, went back inside and lay down. Although the heat of the day made sleep impossible he didn't get up until well into evening, and when he did he was too restless to just sit on the porch. Without making a conscious decision he found himself walking across the field behind the Tourist Court to the county reservoir. It was full dusk when he came upon the lake, deserted now, and saw the raft floating offshore. Evening birds, swallows, were darting back and forth across the lake's surface, the water black and dead calm. At the water's edge he sat down on a large boulder.

I thought you told me you already could swim.

Not for-real swimming.

A small raccoon wandered down to the water near where the old man sat quietly. It dug among the rocks on the shore for several minutes, looking for crawfish, before realizing the old man was there. It froze for an instant, and then, somehow recognizing that it was in no danger, sat up on its hind legs to see better in the rapidly fading light. It chittered once, twice, and then turned from the lake, troubled by something it could not understand.

The Rifle

The coffin was aluminum, simple and unadorned. A bitter January wind down from the Cascades swept across the tarmac as the baggage handlers, aided by the kid from the funeral home, horsed the coffin out of the belly of the small plane. One of the men straightened up too soon in the darkness and bumped his head against the cargo door; he cursed loudly. The others, shocked, quickly completed the task of transferring the coffin from the plane to the hearse. The two baggage handlers hurried back to the warmth of the Bend terminal while the driver of the hearse, a high school senior whose father owned the funeral home, settled in behind the wheel to wait for the army lieutenant who was signing forms inside the terminal. When the lieutenant finally got into the hearse the boy began talking almost immediately.

"You're just up from San Francisco aren't you?" he asked, knowing that the lieutenant was. "My name's Wil Bennet."

The lieutenant nodded. "Mason," he said without offering to shake hands. "Bill Mason."

As they drove into town Wilford glanced in the rearview mirror to make sure that the coffin was riding securely. He cleared his throat. "Most everyone around here knew Artie," he said.

"Artie?" the lieutenant asked.

Wil cut his eyes over to the lieutenant.

"Oh, you mean Warrant Officer Larsen," Mason said quietly. "Arthur."

"His friends all called him Artie," the boy said.

Wil's father was waiting for them at the funeral home. The three of them unloaded the coffin onto a stainless steel gurney, which Wil and his father, with Lieutenant Mason in tow, rolled into a brightly lit, white-tiled, windowless room.

"The family didn't expect you for another day or two," the father said to the lieutenant. He extended his hand. "The name's Bennet, Tom Bennet."

The lieutenant shook hands. "Pleased to meet you, Mr. Bennet. I'm Bill Mason."

"You've met my boy, Wilford? Out at the airport?"

Mason nodded affirmatively. "Yes, sir."

"I assume you'll be staying through the funeral?" Mr. Bennet asked.

"I don't think so," Mason answered. "My orders are to deliver Warrant Officer Larsen's remains into the custody of the family. Any assistance the next of kin might need with respect to survivor benefits and the like will be provided by the Survivors Assistance Office at Fort Lewis, Washington." Mason stopped and looked at the coffin. "Actually," he continued, "I'd like to leave tomorrow." He looked at his watch. "Today," he corrected, noting that it was well after midnight.

Mr. Bennet looked surprised. "My goodness," he said, "that is a quick return." He cleared his throat, plainly embarrassed. "I believe that Betty and Floyd Larsen, that is, Arthur's folks, thought you would be staying around for several days."

Mason shook his head emphatically. "No, sir," he said, "I can't. My orders are clear. I've got to return to the Presidio of San Francisco as soon as I've delivered Warrant Officer Larsen's remains to the next of kin." Both men were embarrassed now. "I'd like to be able to stay longer," he added, lying, "but I can't."

Mr. Bennet shrugged. "Well," he said, "if you can't, you can't." As the lieutenant had done, he looked at his watch. "You might as well stay with us tonight," he said. "All the motels are closed by now, and there's no sense in paying for a whole night when there's just a few hours left until daylight."

Mason shook his head. "No, sir," he said, "thank you, but I'd better get a motel room. If your boy could give me a lift I'd appreciate it."

"No, really," Mr. Bennet said. "I insist you stay here. We've got a perfectly nice guest room in the family quarters." He looked at his son. "Wilford, get Lieutenant Mason's bag out of the car."

"Leaving today?" Floyd Larsen couldn't believe his ears. He had come down to the funeral home as soon as Tom Bennet called to tell him that the coffin containing his son's remains had arrived early that morning. "How can he leave today? He just got here a few hours ago."

"That's what he said, Floyd." Tom Bennet shook his head sympathetically. "Said the army wants him back as soon as possible."

"That's just not right, Tom, you know that." Floyd worried his moustache with his right hand. "It's not right to bring my boy home and just take off like that."

"It's not the lieutenant's fault, Floyd. He has to obey orders, you know." Tom put his hand on his friend's shoulder. "I'm thinking he feels plenty bad about the whole thing."

Floyd stood up. "I'm calling Bob Watson." Bob Watson was the congressional representative for the district that included the city of Bend. "By God, they're not going to just drop my boy off like a sack of potatoes."

"Floyd," Tom said, "why not wait until you meet the lieutenant. He'll be down in just a minute, and you can talk to him about the situation."

Floyd shook his head and turned to leave. "I'm not waiting for anything or anybody until after I've talked to the congressman."

Shortly after Floyd Larsen left, Bill Mason walked into the kitchen carrying his small overnight bag.

"Good morning, Lieutenant," Tom said. "I hope you slept well."

"Fine," Bill said. "I wonder if I might use your telephone," he said. "I need to call the airport and make arrangements for my flight back to San Francisco."

"Of course," Tom said, "but there's no need to rush. The first flight out to Portland doesn't leave until one-thirty this afternoon. Then there's another one at five after five. Why don't you sit down and have some breakfast? Then you can call."

Reluctantly, Bill sat down. Tom brought toast and coffee to the table.

"Where's your son?" Bill asked, wondering how he would get to the airport.

"He's off to school," Tom answered. "But don't worry, I can give you a ride out to the airport when you're ready to go."

Embarrassed, Bill blushed. He busied himself with pouring cream into his coffee and buttering his toast.

"Floyd Larsen, young Arthur's father, was here not too long ago," Tom said. "He was pretty upset, getting a little hot under the collar, I'm afraid."

Bill looked up. "Is anything wrong?" he asked, suddenly nervous.

"No," Tom replied, "nothing's wrong, leastways nothing you've done. He's unhappy that you're planning to leave right away."

Bill resumed eating, relieved. "I'm sorry about that," he said, "but like I told you last night it's not my doing. The people from over at Fort Lewis will help out now that I've delivered Warrant Officer Larsen's remains."

Tom Bennet shrugged. "I told him that, but you have to understand that Arthur is, was, Floyd's only son, his only child." Tom placed his coffee cup on the counter. "Anyway, that's between you and him."

Bill quickly finished his breakfast and stood up. "I'd like to use that telephone now," he said, "if you don't mind."

"You bet," Tom said. "You can use the one in my office."

After several minutes Bill rejoined Tom in the kitchen. "Well it's all set," he said, relief evident in his voice. "I'm booked on the 1:30 flight to Portland and on to San Francisco. If you wouldn't mind giving me a lift out there now, I'll be out of your hair."

"Don't be silly," Tom said. "I wouldn't think of having you sit out at that airport for five hours. You just make yourself comfortable here, and I'll run you out there with plenty of time to spare."

By ten o'clock it seemed to Bill that he had been trapped at the Bennet Funeral Home for several days.

"Excuse me." Tom Bennet's sudden appearance startled Bill out of his reverie. "You have a phone call."

"A phone call?" Bill repeated.

"Yes," Tom said, "you can take it in my office."

The telephone conversation was one-sided and short. Bill listened intently, unconsciously nodding his head once or twice. "Shit," he hissed as he hung up the phone.

"Anything wrong?" Tom asked.

Bill turned to face him. "No, sir," he said. "I've been ordered by my commanding officer to stay here in Bend until
after Warrant Officer Larsen's funeral."

"Well, I wouldn't worry too much about it," Tom said,
trying to cheer the young lieutenant up. "Floyd and Betty
will feel much better just having someone from the army
around. Oh, and I'm sure Roslyn, Arthur's wife, will too."

Bill shook his head. "I don't know what I can do," he said,
more to himself than to Tom. "The people from Fort Lewis
would be so much better. They know all about the survivors' benefits and like that."

"You won't have to do a thing," Tom said. "Just being
here will be enough. Remember, you brought their boy
home to them."

"How soon do you suppose the funeral will be?" Bill asked
hopefully.

"Well," Tom answered, pulling on his lower lip, "let's
see. Today is Tuesday. The Larsens have relatives over near
La Grande, south of Pendleton, most of whom I expect will
want to come to the funeral." Tom nodded, his mind already
full of the details he would be expected to deal with. He
looked at Bill. "I'm thinking Friday."

"Friday?" Bill's response was almost a groan. "I only
brought one extra shirt with me," he said. "And where will I
stay for that long?"

Tom put his hand on the young man's shoulder. "You're
the one that brought young Arthur home. Folks know that.
Why don't you let me worry about the details?"

Tom's assistant knocked softly on the door. "Sorry to interrupt, Tom, but the Larsens are in the chapel," she said.

Tom nodded and turned to Bill. "Why don't you wait here," he said. "I'll go and talk to Floyd and Betty for a few minutes and then bring them back here to meet you."

In less than ten minutes Tom was back with the Larsens.

"Lieutenant Mason," Tom adopted a rather formal tone for the introductions, "this is Mr. and Mrs. Larsen. Arthur's parents," he added unnecessarily.

Floyd Larsen took Bill's hand in a strong grip and looked him over carefully. "Lieutenant," he said, still gripping his hand, "my wife and I would like to thank you for bringing our boy home to us." He paused and looked at his wife. "We know that this isn't a pleasant thing for you to have to do." He indicated Tom Bennet with a nod of his head. "I understand that you haven't a place to stay. Mother..." another nod, this one in the direction of his wife, "...and I want you to stay with us."

Bill didn't say anything.

"It's settled then." Floyd took the young lieutenant's silence for assent and finally, almost regretfully, released his hand. He turned to his wife. "Mother," he said, "perhaps you'd be more comfortable in the chapel while I speak with Tom here and the lieutenant." His eyes guided his wife out of the office. As soon as she was gone, he closed the door. "Tom," he said, "I'd like to see Arthur now."

Tom Bennet was prepared. "Floyd," he said, his voice lowered in respect, "I'm going to have to advise you against that." He went to his desk and withdrew a sheaf of paperwork from the top drawer. "Lieutenant Mason brought these documents with him. They're from the army's Mortuary and Graves Registration Unit at the Oakland Army Base." He handed Floyd one of the documents. Printed in bold letters across its front was the warning "Remains Not Suitable for Viewing."

"I don't care what it says there," Floyd said, "I've got to be sure."

"Floyd," Tom said, his hand on his friend's shoulder, "believe me, you don't want to do this. The army has determined that these are Arthur's remains. That's all you and Betty need to know. Let's do what these papers tell us to do and hold a closed-casket service."

Floyd shook off Tom's hand. "I'll see my son now," he said, his tone of voice precluding further counsel or argument. "I'll see him now."

Tom looked to Bill for support and found the young lieutenant staring fixedly out the window at the colorless winter sky. Tom turned back to Floyd. "All right," he said, "but I wish you wouldn't." He glanced in Bill's direction. "Would you like to accompany us?" he asked.

Bill continued to stare out the window, afraid that by even watching the conversation he would be somehow drawn further into the anguish permeating the room. He shook his head silently, and only when he heard the two men leave the room did he turn around, his heart pounding with dread. He reached inside his uniform blouse and pulled out a pack of cigarettes. The very act of lighting up had a calming effect, the familiar click-clack of the Zippo like the voice of an old

and trusted friend. There was no ashtray on the desk or anywhere else in the office that he could see, so with a quick
look at the door he dropped the ash from his cigarette onto
the shag carpeting, grinding it in with his gleaming brogan.
Before he could finish the cigarette Tom and Floyd returned.
Floyd was pale and tight-lipped.

"We'll take Mother home now," he said.

"Lieutenant?"

Bill awoke to Floyd's muted but insistent voice coming
through the bedroom door.

"Lieutenant?" Floyd again. "Are you awake? It's almost
eight o'clock."

"Yes, sir," Bill answered, "I'm awake."

Arthur's bed was too short for Bill and the mattress too
soft. It had been a dreadfully long night, full of dreams and
visitations.

"Did you sleep well?" Floyd asked at the breakfast table.

Bill sipped a cup of weak coffee, almost like tea. "Yes,
sir," he said.

Floyd nodded. "Mother doesn't feel like getting up and
about just yet, so I figured you and I would go out for a bite
to eat." Floyd looked at the uniform Bill was wearing. "If I
might make a suggestion, why don't you change clothes?"

Bill shook his head. "Unfortunately, sir, this uniform is all
I have with me."

Floyd nodded. "I know," he said. "But you and Arthur are
almost the same size. Why don't you put on something of
his?"

"I don't know," Bill said, uncertain how to respond. "Maybe I better not."

"Nonsense," Floyd said, rising from the table, "Arthur wouldn't mind. I thought you might enjoy getting out and seeing some of the country around Bend, and there's no sense in getting your good uniform all messed up."

Fifteen minutes later Bill rejoined Floyd in the kitchen. He was dressed in blue jeans and a Pendleton wool shirt. Floyd smiled.

"That's just perfect," he said, "just perfect."

They had breakfast at a diner near the center of Bend and were interrupted repeatedly by men stopping by their table to shake Floyd's hand and offer condolences.

"This is Lieutenant Mason," Floyd said as he introduced Bill. "He brought my boy Arthur home." The men all shook Bill's hand. "The lieutenant's just back from Vietnam himself," Floyd added proudly.

Bill said nothing, just nodded and smiled.

After breakfast, Floyd drove to his brother's home. "You didn't meet Eugene yesterday because he couldn't get off work," Floyd explained to Bill. "Eugene runs a big maintenance and repair facility for Detroit Diesel, and he was on the road doing a job over in Deschutes. I told him we'd drop by after breakfast."

Eugene Larsen had converted his garage into a lounge of sorts, with a pool table and a refrigerator that he had fitted out as a draft beer dispenser, complete with a tap mounted on the outside of the door. He was a large, heavyset man with scarred, arthritic-looking hands.

"Welcome to Bend, son," he told Bill. "I know this ain't the most pleasant of circumstances but I can't tell you how much I and everyone else around here appreciate what you done, bringing Arthur home and all."

Despite the early hour, Eugene insisted they all have a beer. "Have a seat," he said, looking at Bill. "I understand you're from North Carolina. You do much hunting?"

Bill sat down. "Yes, sir," he said. "I used to hunt a bit."

"Deer?" Eugene asked.

Bill took a drink of beer and shook his head. "Birds mostly. Lot of quail and dove. Some rabbit and squirrel." He lit a cigarette. "I've never hunted deer."

"Too bad you're not going to be here longer," Eugene said, finishing his beer in one long swallow, "or we'd get you a buck."

"Thought maybe the three of us'd go out and do a little shooting this morning," Floyd said. "What do you think?"

It took Bill a second to realize that the question had been directed at him. He looked first at Eugene and then Floyd. "Well, sure," he said, "whatever."

They drove east out of Bend, toward the mountains. Fifteen miles out of town, Floyd drove his car off the road and onto a vast range of scrub bush and hardpan. A mile from the road they stopped at the base of a large piñon pine. Several rough shooting stands had been nailed together using scrap two-by-fours and plywood, and, some two hundred yards downrange, Bill could see three large target boards standing. The ground surrounding the shooting stands was littered with brass cartridge casings.

"Arthur and I used to come out here all the time," Floyd said as he slid a rifle out of a soft leather carrying case.

Eugene, standing off to one side, nodded. "That boy loved to shoot," he added. "Got his first buck when he was twelve years old."

Floyd handed the rifle to Bill. "That's a Marlin 30/30," he said. "Gave it to Arthur as a Christmas present eight years ago."

Bill hefted the smallish, lever-action rifle, cracking the lever to ensure that it was unloaded. He sighted down the barrel toward the target stands. "Feels good," he said, handing it back to Floyd.

Floyd took the rifle and began mounting a telescopic sight. Eugene walked over to where Bill and Floyd were standing and flourished a large revolver. He aimed it at an empty beer can lying on the ground some thirty feet away and fired one round. The big gun jumped in his hand, and a booming report rolled across the empty plain. The beer can disappeared in a large cloud of dirt kicked up by the bullet. When the dust settled the can reappeared, obviously unhit. Eugene turned and smiled at Bill.

"This here's a man's gun," he said, offering it to Bill. "Iver Johnson, .44 Magnum. Ever fire one before?"

Bill shook his head. "Can't say as I have," he said. He raised and cocked the heavy piece in one, expert motion and fired at the same can Eugene had missed. When the bullet hit it, it jumped at least six feet into the air, spinning end over end. A second dull boom rolled toward the Cascades.

"You two quit messing around," Floyd called out, the

business of mounting the scope completed. "Eugene, run the car on down and put up a couple of fresh targets. Bill, you come on over here and see what you think of this."

Bill carefully handed the revolver back to Eugene and walked over to the shooting stand where Floyd was loading the Marlin.

"Last time Arthur and I fired out here he had the scope sighted in right on two hundred yards," Floyd said. He pointed downrange to where Eugene was stapling fresh paper targets onto two of the target boards. "Those targets are exactly two hundred yards from this bench."

Bill and Floyd stood quietly waiting for Eugene to return. As soon as he was back, Bill walked over to the shooting stand. He leaned onto the stand and placed the Marlin's stock against his right cheek. The sharp, sweet smell of solvent and linseed oil rose from the weapon and evoked an almost hallucinatory image in his mind of young men firing automatic weapons into dense undergrowth, the ejected cartridges whirring through the air like startled birds flushed from underfoot. Squinting through the scope he saw the fresh targets. Behind him, both Eugene and Floyd observed the targets through binoculars. Bill relaxed his shoulders, held his breath, and squeezed the trigger. A hole appeared in the target, an inch left and two inches high of the bull's-eye. Bill stared through the scope for a second and levered a fresh round into the chamber. Again he relaxed, stilled his breathing, and fired. A second hole appeared, just touching the first. He closed both eyes and inhaled deeply, his mouth slightly open, tasting the aroma of the smokeless powder on his lips and tongue. Floyd and Eugene watched silently as Bill straightened up and made a small adjustment to the scope's settings. Taking the rifle up once again he snugged it onto his cheek and settled the crosshairs on the target. Lost completely in ritual he fired the remaining three rounds in the rifle's magazine without conscious thought. He knew without looking, even as he knew his own name, that all three bullets had pierced the target's bull's-eye. An aching sadness settled over his shoulders as he stared downrange through the rifle's scope, his life reduced, it seemed, to mere holes in a paper target. *I feel like an old man*, he thought, *an old man, and I don't know why.* He laid the rifle on the stand and began to cry, tears rolling off his cheeks and onto the Marlin's walnut stock. Floyd and Eugene looked at each other and, embarrassed for the young lieutenant, stood discreetly away from him. After several minutes Eugene reached into the glove box of his car and took out a pint bottle of bourbon. He walked over and wordlessly offered it to Bill.

Later, in the car, Eugene finally spoke. "That was some mighty fine shooting back there," he said, eyeing Bill through the rearview mirror.

Bill nodded his head but did not reply.

"How long were you in Vietnam?" Roslyn asked from the kitchen where she was putting on a pot of coffee.

Bill sat nervously on the edge of the sofa, his hands busily looking for something to do with themselves. He had been having lunch with Floyd and Betty on Thursday when Tom

Bennet called to tell him that Roslyn, Arthur's wife, wanted to meet with him.

"Mother and I did not approve of Arthur's getting married," Floyd told Bill as he drove him over to Roslyn's house. "They ran off to Portland and got married without our consent. She's older than Arthur." Floyd pulled up in front of the house. "It broke Mother's heart."

Bill said nothing, dreading being left alone with another man's widow.

Roslyn sat down next to him on the sofa. "The coffee'll be ready directly," she said. "I'll bet you're happy to be back."

"One year," Bill said, looking down at his hands.

"Pardon me?" Roslyn asked.

"You asked how long I was in Vietnam," Bill said. "One year. The standard tour of duty."

"Artie was only there five months," Roslyn said quietly.

Bad fucking luck, Bill thought.

Roslyn suddenly stood up. "How do you take your coffee?" she asked.

"Black'll be fine," Bill answered, wondering how long he would have to stay with Roslyn that afternoon.

Roslyn disappeared into the kitchen. After a minute she reappeared in the doorway. "I burned the coffee," she said. "How about a drink?"

Bill had never heard of anyone burning coffee before. "What are you having?" he asked.

"I'm going to have a glass of wine," she answered, "but I've got beer, too."

"Beer's fine," Bill said, still curious about the coffee.

Roslyn joined him on the sofa with a large glass of white wine and a bottle of Olympia beer. "Artie and his friends used to collect the Oly bottle caps," she said to Bill. "Guys in Oregon say that if a fellow finds a cap with three dots printed on the inside he can give it to a girl and she has to give him a piece of pussy."

Bill, shocked, closely examined the label on his bottle of beer in order to avoid looking at Roslyn.

"Are you married?" Roslyn asked.

"No," Bill replied, "I'm not."

"Girlfriend?"

Bill continued to stare at the Olympia label on his beer bottle. He shook his head.

"Another beer?" Roslyn asked.

Bill looked up. Roslyn had already finished her glass of wine.

"I'm going to have another glass of wine," she said. "Would you like another beer?"

"No," Bill said, "I've still got some left." He had not yet taken a drink.

Roslyn walked out to the kitchen and reappeared a few seconds later, glass full. "You don't mind if I have another one, do you?" she asked.

"No," Bill said quickly, "not at all."

"Artie and I didn't really know each other for too long before we got married," Roslyn said. She sat down next to Bill on the sofa. "My family's from up near Redmond. Right after we got married Artie enlisted for helicopter school." She took a drink of her wine. "I only saw Artie twice before he went off to Vietnam. He got two weeks' leave after basic training and then a week before he left the country." Roslyn shook her head, puzzled. "Other than that it was just letters." She laughed. "He wanted me to write every day but only wrote me himself every couple of weeks. After the first month I couldn't think of anything to write. Actually, I never missed him all that much." She looked over at Bill. "You must think I'm awful, saying a thing like that with Artie dead and all."

Bill didn't know what to say.

"His folks hate me, you know," Roslyn continued. "His mother already told me she didn't want me to come to the funeral. They think I stole their little Arthur away from them." Roslyn paused and looked at Bill. "Do you think I'm attractive?"

The sudden question caught Bill by surprise. Before he could think he nodded affirmatively.

"As soon as I get the insurance money from the government I'm going to move to San Francisco," Roslyn said. "Or Los Angeles. Any place but here." She finished her glass of wine.

"Do you want the flag?" Bill asked suddenly.

"What flag?" Roslyn asked. "Are you ready for another beer now?"

Bill put the bottle of beer he had been holding on the table. "No, no thank you. Your husband's casket will be draped with an American flag at the funeral. Afterwards, after the casket is lowered into the ground, I've got to present the flag to his next of kin. That's you." Bill paused for a moment. "The only problem is that Mrs. Larsen, Warrant Officer Larsen's mother, wants the flag. Mr. Larsen told me this morning."

"Got a cigarette?" Roslyn asked. Bill gave her one and lit it for her. "What did you tell him?" she asked.

"I told him that if you wanted the flag I would have to give it to you, but that I could probably get another one sent over from Fort Lewis for them." Bill cleared his throat, embarrassed. "Do you want the flag?"

"If that doesn't beat all," Roslyn said. "A flag." She shook her head. "A goddamn flag." She got up and walked back into the kitchen for another glass of wine. "You know," she said when she was once again seated next to Bill, "I doubt that Artie and I would have made it for very long if he'd gotten back alive." She shrugged. "There just wasn't enough there, between us, to keep us going. Still, there should be more left of Artie for me to hold onto than just a flag, you know?"

Outside, dusk was hastened by an approaching weather front. Bill sat quietly and watched the first snowflakes swirl around the window. Neither of them spoke for the longest time.

"Would you do me a favor?" Roslyn finally asked, not looking at Bill. "Would you stay with me for a while, and let's not talk about Artie or his parents or flags or anything like that." Roslyn took one of Bill's hands into her own and held it tightly. "Would you do that for me?"

Long after the eastern Oregon sky had blackened into night the two of them sat on the sofa holding hands in the dark, neither rising to turn on a light.

"Mother and I were worried when you didn't return last night," Floyd said to Bill. The two men were sitting at the breakfast table at the Larsens' house. Betty was nowhere to be seen.

"I'm sorry, sir, I didn't mean to worry you," Bill said. "What with the storm and all, I thought it best to stay at Mrs. Larsen's house." He looked down at his cup of coffee.

Floyd paused for a moment, a frown creasing his brow. "Did you speak with her about the flag?"

"Yes, sir, I did," Bill replied. "My impression was that she would like to have the flag."

"Did you tell her of the flag's significance to Arthur's mother?" Floyd asked.

"I told her that she was entitled to the flag as Warrant Officer Larsen's next of kin and that if she didn't want it that you and your wife did." Bill rose from the breakfast table. "If you'll excuse me, I have to return Mrs. Larsen's car to her and get over to Mr. Bennet's." He hesitated for a brief second, wanting to say more, but not knowing how.

"What did they say?" Roslyn asked. She was driving Bill to the Bennet Funeral Home.

"Nothing," Bill said, knowing what she meant.

"I don't believe that," Roslyn said with a laugh. "Never mind, though, you don't have to tell me. I already know what they think about me."

"Have you given any more thought to the flag?" Bill asked.

"Not really," Roslyn said. "What do you think I should do?"

Bill shook his head. "I don't know."

Roslyn stopped at the curb in front of the funeral home and Bill got out. He opened the rear door and grabbed his overnight bag from the back seat. Before he could withdraw it Roslyn reached over the front seat and placed her hand on his arm.

"Thank you for last night," she said.

Bill nodded but didn't say anything.

"I meant what I said about leaving here and maybe moving to San Francisco as soon as I get the insurance money." Roslyn hesitated, afraid to say anything further but more afraid not to. "Do you suppose I might give you a call?"

Bill looked away and shook his head. "I won't be there much longer," he said. "I'll be getting my discharge sometime in the next few weeks and leaving. Going home." He took his overnight bag from the back seat and straightened up, closing the car door behind him. He turned and strode quickly up the walk to the funeral home, pausing only briefly at the door to watch Roslyn drive slowly away.

The funeral was conducted in two parts, the first a religious service held in the small chapel at the funeral home, the second a ceremony at graveside. Bill sat at the rear of the chapel for the eulogy and listened to the wind as it rattled the chapel's ornate double doors. Roslyn sat alone in the first pew on the left side, Floyd and Betty alone in the first pew on the right. Arthur's remains had been transferred from the quartermaster-issue aluminum casket to a dark rosewood-and-mahogany civilian model sold by Tom Bennet. The casket was closed.

After the eulogy the mourners regathered at the cemetery.
The large canopy erected over the gravesite was in such danger of being blown away by the strong wind that Tom stationed employees at each guy rope to provide additional
support. The minister kept his remarks brief, and the coffin
was quickly lowered into the grave. When it reached the bottom, Bill stepped forward with the folded American flag. He
stood in front of Roslyn and placed it in her hands. Roslyn
held the flag for a moment, then turned and gave it to Betty.

"That was a nice gesture out there with the flag, don't you
think?" Tom Bennet asked. He and Bill were standing in the
kitchen back at the funeral home, warming themselves with
coffee. Bill had ridden back from the cemetery in the hearse
with Tom. Before he could respond Floyd Larsen appeared
in the doorway.

"Why, hello, Floyd," Tom said, "I didn't realize you were
coming back here."

"I only stopped by for a moment," Floyd said. "Mother's
waiting in the car outside. I'd like to talk to Lieutenant
Mason, if I may."

"Sure, Floyd," Tom said. "Why don't you use my office."

"First," Floyd said, when he and Bill were alone in Tom's
office, "I'd like to thank you for convincing Roslyn to give
Arthur's flag to Mother."

Bill shook his head. "I didn't do anything, sir," he said.
"The decision was hers."

"I don't believe that," Floyd said, "and neither does
Mother. What you did meant a great deal to Mother, and we

both thank you. Secondly, I want you to have this." He held up the leather carrying case that Bill knew contained Arthur's rifle.

"No, sir," Bill said, shaking his head vehemently, "I can't accept that. It's against regulations."

"You have to take it," Floyd said. "I saw the way you fired it the other day. You were made for this rifle. Just like Arthur was. He'd want you to have it. He'd insist on it."

Bill put his hands up, refusing to take the gift. "I'm sorry, sir," he said, "I just can't. There must be someone else in your family who would want it, and anyway, like I said, I'd be breaking the law by taking it. I could be court-martialed if someone found out."

Floyd shook his head, oblivious to what Bill was saying. He was smiling and crying at the same time, a sight that unnerved the young lieutenant. "Arthur wants you to have it," he kept saying, forcing the leather case into Bill's hands. "Please take it, for Mother's sake, and mine. It will mean so much to us, knowing that Arthur's rifle is in your hands."

He thrust the rifle bag into Bill's arms and then abruptly turned and left the office. Tom Bennet came in a few seconds later. He laid an arm on Bill's shoulder. "I kind of thought Floyd was going to do something like this. You did the right thing," he said, nodding in the direction of the case Bill was holding.

When the flight from Bend to Portland left at five minutes after five that afternoon, the sun was almost gone from the sky. Bill was the only passenger in the twin-engine Cessna, and he sat directly behind the pilot, the rifle bag clutched between his knees. He bought a cup of coffee in Portland and sat down to wait for his connecting flight. When the flight was finally called, he rose and walked directly to the large men's room opposite the boarding gate. Two men were standing at the urinals when he entered, and Bill waited quietly near the door until they both left, the last one out giving him a rather quizzical sidelong glance. As soon as he was alone, Bill lifted the rifle bag and thrust it savagely into the large trash can that stood in the center of the tiled restroom. An almost uncontrollable urge to laugh came over him as he ran, stumbling, from the restroom to the boarding gate.

"You almost missed the flight, sir," the ticket agent said to him with a frown as he handed her his ticket. "You're the last one on board."

Spanky's Dead

~

"Dead?" Incredulous, little Jimmy Ledger jumped to his feet. "What the fuck are you talking about?"

Five or six of the boys were hanging around Claude McCutcheon's bunk in the third platoon's barracks. It was a little after eight o'clock in the PM when JoJo Watson, a nineteen-year-old freckled redhead from Monmouth, New Jersey, announced to one and all that Spanky, child star of the Our Gang comedies, had recently expired.

"Just what I said. The motherfucker's dead." Pleased that his statement had created such a stir, at least in Ledger's case, JoJo paused dramatically to light a cigarette, opening his Zippo with a flourish and snapping it shut again with a flip of his thumb. Peering up at Ledger through the smoke, JoJo added insult to injury. "I think he died of syphilis or something like that." JoJo carefully deposited the ash from his cigarette into an empty Kiwi tin sitting next to him on McCutcheon's footlocker. "All those Hollywood guys are queers."

Ledger was so agitated that he couldn't stand still. He pointed an accusing finger at JoJo. "Oh, yeah? Well, you don't know jackshit. Spanky wasn't no queer."

"Son," JoJo shook his head sadly, indicating to the rest of the boys with upturned palms how badly he felt that Ledger was so ignorant, "if you'd get your nose out of those goddamn books you're reading all the time you'd know what the hell I'm talking about. The sonofabitch is dead, and that's all there is to it."

Frustrated by JoJo's cool demeanor, Ledger could think of no response. "Well, I don't believe it." He turned to Percy Martin. "Do you believe it?"

Martin, a taciturn West Virginian, shook his head. "Man, I don't know nothing about no goddamn Spanky."

Martin's denial astounded Ledger even more than JoJo's pronouncement of death. He walked away from the group shaking his head, carefully skirting the highly polished linoleum center strip of the squad bay. Laughter followed him.

"Now that's just what I'm talking about." JoJo looked around. "An education don't mean shit when you got no common sense."

The conversation paused momentarily but no one was inclined to leave, for there was little else to do. With payday still five days away, none of the boys had sufficient cash to go to the enlisted men's club for beer.

"Hey!" JoJo suddenly thought of something. "How about

that sonofabitch over at Bravo Company that got run over by
the APC yesterday?"

The boys brightened up, for here was a topic with consid-
erable promise. A young soldier with one of the other com-
panies in the their training brigade had been killed by an
armored personnel carrier, a tracked vehicle used to move
troops rapidly around a battlefield. The unfortunate man's
company had been practicing combat assaults and somehow
or other in all the excitement he had gotten himself run
over.

"Bad fucking luck," murmured Floyd Bannerman, a tall,
thin private from Iowa, or *Io-fucking-way* as it was pronounced throughout the squad bay.

"Fuckin' A," agreed Jim Burke, standing next to him.

All the boys nodded in agreement and several unconsciously grabbed their crotches as they imagined what a body
run over by an APC must look like.

"I hate those fucking PCs," JoJo said. "It's like riding
around in a goddamn coffin. And another thing," JoJo paused
and made sure he had everyone's attention. "How about that
goddamn Will Penny?"

JoJo was referring to the title character of the movie then
playing at the theater annex adjacent to the battalion's barracks. Percy Martin, who had already seen the film three
times was moved to uncharacteristic volubility.

"I'd have never left that woman," he said.

"I don't know," said Bull Harper, a diminutive recruit
from Baltimore, still focused on the untimely demise of his
comrade-in-arms. "How could the APC's driver have just

backed over him like that?" The Bull looked at JoJo. "I don't like it," he said. "I don't like it, and I don't even want to think about it."

Unfortunately, now that the topic had been raised, the Bull *would* think about it. All night.

"The thing is, it's probably not such a bad way to go." JoJo said, hoping to needle the Bull further. "I mean, it couldn't have hurt very much, could it?" He looked around. "At least not for long."

Suddenly, Floyd Bannerman straightened up as if he'd been stuck with a pin.

"Sonofabitch," he said excitedly, "I almost forgot. Mr. Abrams, down at the motor pool, is going in to the dispensary to get circumcised next week."

Even JoJo was struck temporarily dumb. Floyd quickly pressed his advantage.

"Give me a cigarette," he said to JoJo, "and I'll tell you guys about it."

JoJo was so astonished that he passed over his pack without thinking. Floyd lit up and exhaled dramatically through his nose.

"I ain't shitting you, Abrams is getting circumcised next week. He told Sergeant Ford about it, and Ford told Buddy Sims about it, and Buddy told me." Floyd took a quick drag and continued. "Today. Right after motor stables. A goddamn circumcision."

Mr. Abrams was the warrant officer who ran the battalion's motor pool, and Sergeant Ford was the battalion maintenance NCO. Every week one of the battalion's platoons was detailed to spend a day on so-called motor stables, help-ing the maintenance platoon perform routine preventive maintenance on the battalion's motor vehicles.

"I've heard some silly shit in my day, but this has to beat all." JoJo looked disgusted. "What in the fuck is a grown man doing getting a goddamn circumcision for?" He looked around. "Now you know that's got to hurt."

The Bull was confused. "What's a circumcision?" he wanted to know.

Everybody laughed. JoJo was beside himself. When some-one calmed down long enough to describe the procedure to him, the Bull quickly grabbed his crotch, his eyes wide.

"Jesus Christ, Bull, in all the fucking latrines you been in you ain't never noticed that some guys' dicks look different than others?" JoJo asked.

Shocked that someone would think he looked at other men's private parts, the Bull quickly denied any knowledge of comparative anatomy.

"I don't believe it," said Howard Fuller. "Ain't no way no grown man is going to get the head of his dick cut off."

"It ain't the head, it's just the skin around it," Floyd coun-tered. "Besides, Sergeant Ford said so, and he heard it direct from Mr. Abrams."

"Shit." Howard, unimpressed, worked a toothpick around the corner of his mouth. "Sergeant Ford'll tell you any god-damn thing. Why'd he say he was doing it?"

Floyd was defensive, annoyed that his revelation was being met with skepticism. "Buddy said that Ford said that

Abrams's new wife wants him to. Said she liked the feel of a circumcised dick better."

The boys cracked up, and immediately fell to an animated discussion of the relative merits of circumcision versus non-circumcision. Ultimately, the vote as to which was better split along predictable lines. As the topic was winding down, Sergeant Erskine Wilson, the platoon's drill sergeant, walked into the squad bay. A seventeen-year army veteran, Wilson had fought in Korea and had already served one tour in the 'Nam.

"Listen up, you miserable lobcocks," he yelled, clearly intoxicated. "I just got another letter from Clyde."

Sergeant Wilson's younger brother Clyde, a staff sergeant, was serving as an adviser to a South Vietnamese paratroop regiment. Clyde's letters to Erskine, usually filled with graphic descriptions of ceaseless combat, were of great interest to the boys in the platoon.

"Got a letter from Clyde this morning," Sergeant Wilson repeated, waving the subject letter in his right hand for emphasis. "Figured you dickbrains would want to hear about all the shit you'll be stirring around in shortly." Wilson paused as he fumbled with the letter, struggling to get it out of its envelope. "Goddamn it," he cursed, finally tearing it free. "Listen to this." He glared around at his audience with the fiery-eyed stare of a Pentecostal preacher. "'We just got back from a search-and-destroy operation in the central highlands, up near Pleiku. We were wandering all over the fucking place freezing our tits off—'"

"Freezing?" Little Jimmy Ledger had wandered back to the group. "I thought it was hot over there."

Sergeant Wilson shook his head with the authority of one who knew. "Not up in the highlands. Not in the winter." He cleared his throat and almost spit on the floor. "Now listen. 'As usual, the South Vietnamese outfit spent all their time trying to avoid any contact with the VC.'"

JoJo shook his head. "I don't know why we even fuck around with them. They ought to just get out of the way and let us fight the goddamn war."

Sergeant Wilson was annoyed that his narrative had yet again been interrupted. "Did I ask you for your goddamn opinion, private?"

"No, drill sergeant," JoJo meekly replied.

"Well, then, shut the fuck up." Wilson glared about, daring anyone else to interrupt him. "As I was saying," he continued, "'We got overrun the last night out. The fucking perimeter guards they put out were asleep, or dicking off, or something, and the shit hit the fan. The VC dropped a few mortar rounds in to shake things up and then charged the perimeter. It was raining and blacker than a well digger's ass, so we couldn't call in air support nor evac neither. It was every swinging dick for himself.'"

The boys were impressed, each trying to imagine himself in such circumstances, small arms fire crackling to every side, willy peter and HE mortar rounds falling closer and closer, battle joined hand-to-hand.

"'It was a goddamn Chinese fire drill. We fought off and on, mostly on, until daylight, when the major commanding the South Vietnamese regiment called for evacuation. I wanted him to reestablish command and control and go after the VC, but he refused and loaded his sorry ass on the first chopper out. I stayed to the end, trying to make sure we weren't leaving any wounded troopers behind.'"

Each of the boys vowed silently never to be captured alive.

Floyd spoke up. "How short is your brother getting, drill sergeant?"

The drill sergeant reached over and grabbed one of JoJo's cigarettes, lighting it with his own lighter. "Short enough. I think he's got only two more months to go on this tour. But I think he's planning to extend for six months. He likes working for MACV. Says he doesn't have to put up with a lot of chickenshit from the brass. Plus, I suspect he's got himself a little mama-san he hates to leave, if you get my point."

"Shit." JoJo shifted on the footlocker as if its surface had suddenly gotten warm.

Sergeant Wilson laughed. "At Ben Cat, with the First, we used to get a steam job and a blow bath almost every day, not counting when we were in the field."

"Did you guys wear rubbers?" Floyd asked. He had heard some ugly stories about an incurable Asian strain of venereal disease from a medic over at the dispensary.

The boys burst out laughing at his question. Sergeant Wilson walked away shaking his head in disgust, astounded at the very thought.

"Floyd, answer me something," JoJo said. "Did your mother have any children that lived?"

"Fuck you," Floyd responded, embarrassed at being laughed at. "You guys won't think it's so funny when your dicks fall off." He walked away slowly, so that no one would think he was leaving because he had asked a dumb question. General laughter prevailed as the boys drifted away to get ready for lights out.

The Ice Machine

"Why do you suppose you drink so much?" the social worker from the Buncombe County court asked me once. I had to laugh at that.

"Hell," I told her, "I do it because I like getting drunk."

Rakoczy liked getting drunk, too. And when he got drunk he liked to fight. In fact, if he hadn't been killed in Vietnam I doubt his career in the army would have gone very far, given his behavior stateside once he'd had a few drinks.

He was my company commander at Fort Bragg, with the 82nd Airborne, and I can still hear his voice, can still see him swaggering into the dayroom or one of the squad bays, but I cannot, as I sit here, summon up his face. For the longest time I thought maybe it was all the drinking I used to do, but now I believe it's just the way the mind works. Like a photograph left in the sun, first the colors and then the image itself just fade away.

I loved Captain Rakoczy like a father, and there weren't many nights at Fort Bragg when he got drunk and wild that I wasn't right beside him. When I learned that he'd been killed I felt pretty bad about it. I was in the hospital myself, at Letterman, when I got a package from his wife:

Dear Lieutenant Morton:

I don't know whether or not you are aware of the fact that James was killed in action almost three months ago. If not, I apologize for having to notify you in this manner. Several of your letters to him were among his personal belongings returned to me after his death. It was only with some difficulty that I got your temporary address at Letterman General Hospital where I understand that you are yourself recuperating from wounds you received in Vietnam. James often spoke to me of his platoon leaders and, at Fort Bragg, the one he spoke most often of was you. I am enclosing with this letter his wristwatch because he used to laugh at the way you admired it without ever saying so. I know that he would have wanted you to have it.

Yours truly,
Maya Rakoczy

She was right about me lusting after that watch. It was an old Rolex, a watch that was something of a talisman or icon among soldiers. I remember Rakoczy telling me once that it had belonged to his father before him, and I can't imagine what his wife was thinking of to give such an heirloom to me.

Anyway, Rakoczy and I had been serving in different units in Vietnam, him with the 173rd and me with the 1st Infantry Division, and so naturally I had not been aware that he had been killed. It was his second tour (my first and only) and, like I said, I doubt he'd have had much of a career in any event. Still, it hit me pretty hard when I got his wife's letter because I can't begin to tell you how much I thought of him.

I spent about three months recuperating at Letterman and then another month waiting for my medical discharge to get processed. It was during that last month, as a transient lieutenant assigned to light duty at Sixth Army Headquarters, that I happened to pull duty officer one night at the Presidio stockade.

"Two more things."

I was sitting in the stockade XO's office being briefed on my responsibilities as overnight duty officer.

"Later this evening," the XO continued, "we'll be transferring a prisoner to the navy brig on Treasure Island. The navy will send three marine guards and a van to pick him up around eight o'clock. When they arrive, you call the TI brig and ask the duty officer there to identify the guards for you while you cross-check the information against their ID cards. You then have the senior guard sign for the prisoner, and you release him to their custody. Note the time of transfer on the duty log, and attach the transfer form, and that's all there is to it."

"Sounds simple enough. How'd you get a sailor in an army stockade?"

The XO smiled. "He's not a sailor. It's a disciplinary matter. These transfers are considered 'sensitive,' so I would advise you not to discuss this outside the sanitary confines of the stockade. The prisoner being transferred, a Private Carbone, has refused to obey lawful orders given him by various members of the guard staff, including myself and the stockade commander, Captain Bartholomew. We have no 'disciplinary facilities' here at the Presidio stockade so problem prisoners are transferred on a temporary basis to the navy brig on TI."

"What's he in for?"

"You name it, he's done it." The XO paused to light a cigarette. "Carbone was drafted in 1967 and properly reported—why, God only knows—for basic training at Fort Dix, New Jersey. On his third day in the army he assaulted a doctor at the base dispensary who interrupted him in the course of an attempted rape of a nurse. He managed to flee the base and worked his way west, ultimately joining a cousin who lives here in San Francisco. Two weeks ago he was arrested by the SFPD following a botched jewelry store holdup. They turned him over to us when the fingerprint checks revealed him to be a deserter. He's waiting here for a general court-martial. Assuming he's convicted, he'll pull hard time at Leavenworth. In the meantime he needs a serious attitude adjustment, and the marines at TI will give him one."

"And the second thing?"

"The second thing is that we've got a prisoner on suicide watch."

"Which means?"

"Which means that you'll have to keep an eye on him all night to make sure he doesn't figure out some way to do himself in."

"What's his problem?"

"His problem is that he's a fucking idiot." The XO ground out his cigarette with a look of disgust. "Unlike Carbone, this asshole Smith actually joined the army of his own free will. He'd finished one year of college before dropping out and visiting his local recruiter. He completed his basic training and was well into AIT when he realized that as an 11Bravo he would shortly be heading across the water to fight the hated Cong. He decided it was time to get right with Jesus." The XO chuckled at his own wit. "So, one dark night he discovered his social conscience and deserted. Fourteen months later he got himself busted here in San Francisco selling marijuana and was shortly thereafter handed over to us by our friends in the SFPD."

"What happens to him now?"

"Here's where it gets interesting. Most of the time these kids like Smith have been getting quick courts, a Bad Conduct Discharge, time served, and 'don't let the doorknob hit you in the ass on the way out.' I guess Sixth Army and the Pentagon figure it's a hell of a lot easier to just boot them, which is what they want anyway. Unfortunately for friend Smith, his court nailed him with a Dishonorable Discharge and two years' hard time at Leavenworth. He was sentenced last week, and he's due to be shipped out to Kansas tomorrow morning. For the last day or two he's been threatening to kill himself."

My right leg, the one the doctors at Letterman told me would permanently be two inches shorter than the left, was aching like a tooth. "Fuck him if he can't take a joke," I said. "Can't you just lock him up in a cell where he can't hurt himself?"

The XO shook his head. "We don't have segregation facilities here. I don't think there's much likelihood Smith actually means to kill himself, but Captain Bartholomew doesn't want to take any chances, particularly with him due to be out of our hair tomorrow. Our attitude is that he can kill himself in Kansas if he wants to, but not here. So, you get to watch him all night."

The stockade building was a smallish, two-story stucco building surrounded by a twenty-foot chain-link fence topped with a triple roll of concertina wire. The first floor contained a barred squad bay capable of holding up to twenty prisoners, a small guard room, and the stockade dispensary. Another twenty-man squad bay was located on the second floor. On the first floor, the MP guards were sending five prisoners at a time downstairs to the basement to get their supper, which they brought back up to the squad bays on standard-issue metal trays. The only sound, other than occasional comments between the guards, was the sibilant shuffling of the prisoners' feet as they walked silently in single file down and up the narrow stairwell to the basement. The basement was a single room, dark and claustrophobic, with a low plaster ceiling and no windows or doors. Meals were not prepared in the stockade but rather brought to it in large field thermos containers and served by two nonprisoner KPs from the garrison mess hall. The scene had a surreal quality about it, the prisoners silently presenting their trays and receiving their allotted portions, taking a cup of coffee or milk, and walking back up the stairs. The servers, anxious to be finished and out of the stockade as quickly as possible, slopped the food onto the trays, never looking at the men they were serving.

Back upstairs, one of the guards, a towheaded kid from the Midwest who couldn't have looked mean if he'd wanted to, spoke to young Joey Carbone, the tough Italian kid bound for the brig on Treasure Island.

"Won't be long now," the guard said, a beatific smile on his face. "The marines from TI should be here in an hour or so."

Carbone, who was seated on the edge of his bunk eating his supper, didn't bother to look up. "Fuck you," he muttered, his mouth full of boiled lima beans.

"I wouldn't talk that way to the guards at TI, if I were you," the young MP advised. "They won't like it."

"Fuck them, too." Joey, pleased with this witty repartee, smirked at his fellow prisoners, about fifteen of them, who were watching and listening to the exchange with some interest. "They better have their lunch with them, because it's going to take a while to get me out of here."

Bold talk, I thought, deciding not to involve myself in the conversation of morons. In the guard room the sergeant of the guard introduced me to Smith, the erstwhile deserter who was threatening to do himself in.

"Sir, this here's Prisoner Smith. You have to keep an eye

on him all night, until you're relieved in the morning by the XO." The sergeant, whose name escapes me after all these years, smiled a hateful smile. "If you'd like, we could do him up in leg irons and manacles for you."

It would have been hard to imagine a young man less in need of leg irons and manacles than Prisoner Smith. Peering out fearfully behind thick glasses was the face of a child and, it seemed to me, despite his alleged year or so of college, not a very bright one. He was tall, six feet or so, and as skinny as a rail. I looked at the big Rolex on my wrist, or rather, at Rakoczy's father's big Rolex. I had only had it then for a couple of months and was always checking the time, so much so that the nurses at Letterman used to laugh at me, saying they doubted I'd ever be late for a date.

"Nice watch," the sergeant said appreciatively.

"Thanks." I looked at Smith. "I'm going to be here at the stockade for approximately the next twelve hours," I told him. "If you think you can avoid harming yourself for that period of time I will allow you to sit here without being chained up like a wild man. Do you suppose you can do that?"

Smith nodded his head gravely up and down.

The sergeant of the guard lashed out his right hand and punched Smith in the chest, a blow that knocked him against the wall of the guard room. "Answer the lieutenant when he talks to you."

"Yessir," Smith stammered, rearranging his glasses back onto the bridge of his nose. "Yessir."

The evening routine at the stockade was a simple one:

after being fed, the prisoners were allowed two hours of so-called free time, during which they could do absolutely nothing except sit around on their bunks and talk quietly. The stockade provided no recreational materials, no radios or television, no books or magazines. This particular evening everyone was waiting with anticipation for the marines from TI, since Prisoner Carbone had vowed to go out fighting. At eight o'clock sharp he got his chance.

"Sir, the men from Treasure Island are here for Prisoner Carbone," the sergeant of the guard informed me.

There were three of them, a lance corporal and two privates first class. I could see from the corporal's ribbons that he had been to Vietnam. It took only a couple of minutes to verify their identities by telephone with the brig duty officer.

"He's all yours," I told the corporal.

"Prisoner Carbone," the Presidio sergeant of the guard yelled, "get your ass out here."

"Fuck you," Carbone yelled from the squad bay, "and the horse you rode in on."

The marines had brought their own leg irons and handcuffs and two of them were carrying hickory billy clubs. The lance corporal smiled slightly upon hearing Carbone's words. It was not a warm smile.

"We'll take care of him," the corporal said.

I'll give Carbone credit, he was a tough little spud. It took the three marines a little longer than they had expected to get him shackled and under control, and in the process Carbone got in a couple of decent licks of his own. In the end, however, they pounded him pretty enthusiastically with the billies, and he had nothing bold to say as they dragged him out.

"He'll be a different man when you get him back," the corporal, breathing heavily, assured the sergeant of the guard, "or either by God we'll kill him one."

"I hope you do kill the sonofabitch," the sergeant responded, caught up in the passion of the moment. I could tell he had badly wanted to get in on the action himself but was inhibited by my presence. He glared around at the other prisoners, hoping one would be so foolish as to say something. None was. "You." The sergeant pointed at Prisoner Smith, standing three feet from me. Smith was pallid and trembling, obviously in great shock from having witnessed Carbone's beating. "Get the mop out of the latrine and clean up this blood, right goddamn now."

Smith leaped to obey the sergeant's shouted order, and seconds later we heard him throwing up in the latrine. The sergeant looked at me and shook his head. "There's no way in hell that dickbrain will survive two years at Leavenworth," he said. "They'll kill him in the first week."

The excitement of Carbone's transfer completed, the hours passed exceedingly slowly. Although I tried not to check the Rolex very often, every time I did it seemed as if only ten or fifteen minutes had passed since the last time I looked. Smith, sitting in a straight-backed wooden chair, kept nodding off to sleep, only to jerk awake when his head fell forward.

"How long has it been since they let you sleep in a bunk?" I asked him. It was just after three in the morning.

The MP guard sitting with us laughed. He was just a private himself, clearly not long out of basic training and AIT. "Since day before yesterday, when he started making those asshole threats about killing himself, ain't that right, Smith?"

"Yessir."

Smith looked and sounded as if his spirit had been worn down to an absolute nub.

"You must of fucked up big-time at your court-martial to get two years at Leavenworth and a Dishonorable while the rest of these bozos," I nodded toward the squad bay where the rest of the prisoners were sound asleep, "are only getting BCDs and a boot," I told him, thinking a little conversation might cheer him up.

Before he could answer, the young MP with us laughed. "He's dead meat," the guard assured me, dismissing Smith's immediate future with a wave of his hand. "Listen, Lieutenant, has anyone shown you the ice machine yet?"

I indicated no.

"Well, hell, sir. It's the only thing in this shit hole," he waved his arm to encompass the entire stockade, "worth seeing. Come on, I'll show it to you." He nodded toward Smith, "Better bring him along."

We walked down the narrow stairs to the basement mess area. There, standing in one corner, was a large, shiny, stainless steel commercial ice machine. At one end was an angled lid with a handle, which provided access to the little ice cubes the machine produced. My guide reached in and grabbed a handful of the geometrically perfect one-inch-square cubes.

"Look at 'em, sir. How the hell do you suppose it makes such perfect little ice cubes?" I merely shrugged my shoulders in reply. He responded with a short, delighted laugh. "How about you, dickhead?" he said to Smith, standing to my rear. "Have you got any idea?" Smith looked as if he couldn't have told anyone with certainty which planet he was on at that moment in time. "Shit," the guard laughed, "nobody ever knows until we show them. Look here."

He flipped a switch and opened the top third of the machine, swinging it up and away on hinges. Expecting the interior space to be jammed with plumbing and complicated wiring, I was suprised to see only a stainless steel shelf running about half the length of the interior and tilted at a shallow angle down toward the end that received and stored the ice cubes. A simple wire grid was suspended over the ice storage area from the lower end of the shelf to the end of the machine. Directly below the grid was the storage area. The guard was unable to contain his delight in my obvious inability to figure out how the little cubes were created.

"Don't feel bad, sir, no one can figure it out at first. Let me show you."

The way it worked was indeed a joy to behold. The slanted shelf had refrigeration tubing built into it, which cooled its surface to below freezing. At the top of the shelf a small perforated copper tube released water, which ran down the length of the shelf. The runoff collected for recirculation in a little trough at the end of the shelf. The running water gradually froze on the shelf, slowly building up a uniform sheet of ice. In the upper right hand corner of the shelf was a small lever, which was pushed upward by the ice as it thickened. When the ice sheet was precisely one inch thick, the lever mechanism sent a signal that shut off the flow of water while simultaneously turning off the cooling mechanism and turning on a heating unit in the shelf. As the shelf warmed, the sheet of ice melted free, slipped off the shelf, and slid onto the wire grid. The grid then received an electrical current, heating the wire to a red-hot incandescence. The ice in direct contact with the wire grid quickly melted, and lo, perfect one-inch-square ice cubes dropped into the storage area. The only moving part was the lever that sensed the thickness of the growing sheet of ice.

"Ain't that something, sir?" The young private looked up at me, his eyes shining in the dim light reflected off the ice machine's stainless steel surface. "I mean, ain't that something to see?"

He told me that throughout the night, while the world slept uneasily, he and his comrades-in-arms frequently slipped down the stairs to the basement to watch the ice machine work its wonders.

"I could watch it for hours," he added as we ascended the stairs from the basement.

It was only about an hour after that that Smith managed to kill himself. I had left him alone, standing more or less at attention, while I went into the latrine to relieve myself. He was in full view of the guard in the guard room and in any event I figured neither he nor I needed him standing next to me while I took a leak. Apparently, as soon as I left him he hotfooted it up the stairs to the second floor and without so much as a final good-bye took a swan dive over the balcony onto the concrete floor below. As luck would have it, he landed head first, which I presume he intended, that being about the only way a person could actually kill himself jumping from just one floor to the next.

Smith's final act of defiance caused me a certain amount of inconvenience, inasmuch as I had to wait around a couple of extra weeks while a board of inquiry conducted an examination into the matter. I have to admit that I was, at the time, underwhelmed by the loss of Prisoner Smith, being as I had just returned from Vietnam. In any event, the board eventually determined that no one was responsible for Smith's death, and I received my medical discharge. I drifted around for a couple of years, never really sticking to anything for too long. I finally ended up back in North Carolina and enrolled in a small teachers' college in Buncombe County, up near Asheville. I got married, had a kid, took to drinking a little too much, and (shades of Prisoner Smith) never did graduate. Still, things have worked out pretty much as well as a fellow could expect. I sell a little life insurance, do some hunting and fishing, and stay mostly sober these days. I miss the army though, I swear I do. I think about it all the time and, surprisingly, I find myself thinking a lot about Prisoner Smith. And being annoyed that I can see his face so clearly and can't for the life of me picture Captain Rakoczy. And the other thing is, I can't get that damned ice machine out of my mind.

Kenny

∾

I thought of Kenny last night. A cold wind soughing through the loblolly pines brought him clearly to mind. Most folks seem to prefer summer or fall, but Kenny and I loved the winter. Mornings we'd get up before dawn and creep out to any one of a dozen ponds, whichever we thought the ducks might come to. It never mattered, not to Kenny nor me, that we seldom shot anything. Just being there, together, was what counted. I mind one morning in particular, so cold the air seemed to sparkle, we watched three mallards come into the small pond out behind Gene Patterson's place. Two hens and a drake, three gray ghosts gliding silently over Gene's curing barn and down to the water like the hand of God settling onto Johnston County. I looked at Kenny and he was crying, tears rolling down his cheeks, a sight that scared me so bad I almost swallowed my chew.

"Lord, Billy," he told me, "I don't believe I want to live anymore."

He didn't either. We backed out of the bushes next to the pond and walked back to the car. We never said another word, just broke the shotguns down and walked out. Later that day, on towards evening, Kenny killed himself. Only three people came to the funeral: me and Ike Farrel and a girl we had gone to high school with and hadn't seen in close to twenty years. She said she had always liked Kenny and came because she saw the death notice in the paper.

"Why do you suppose he done it?" Ike asked me.

Ike hadn't been with us in Vietnam and I didn't want him thinking Kenny was crazy. "I don't rightly know," I said. "I guess it was like that old pig of your daddy's when the ice water hit her. He just didn't have no choice."

When we were kids, Kenny could always think of the damnedest things. We'd been standing around with Ike on a hot August afternoon looking at Ike's daddy's prize sow. The three of us couldn't have been more than thirteen or fourteen. The pig, which must have weighed at least three hundred pounds, was sleeping in the sparse shade of the fence surrounding her pen.

"What'll you reckon would happen if we dumped a bucket of ice water on her?" Kenny asked.

Ike giggled at Kenny's question. "Shoot," he said, "I'd love to see that. Where could we get us any ice?"

Kenny had already figured it out. "Billy can run down to the Esso station on his bike and pick up a five-pound bag."

Twenty minutes later we were ready.

"How hot do you reckon it is?" Ike asked as all of us tried and failed to mentally calculate the effect of ice water on a hot pig.

"It's got to be ninety-five at least," Kenny whispered over his shoulder, concerned lest we wake the pig. "Plus," he added, "the humidity's way up there."

The pig, whose name if memory serves was Betsy, slumbered away, snoring loudly. When Kenny reached the top of the fence, Ike handed him the bucket, and he immediately emptied it on the pig below. The result was catastrophic and satisfying beyond our wildest dreams. When the ice water hit her, Betsy gave forth with a loud squeal and jumped up several feet into the air. Upon landing she fell over onto her side and lay motionless, eyes open and snout quivering. After a second or two she sighed loudly and closed her eyes, quite obviously dead. The three of us were stunned.

"Goddamn," Kenny said, speaking for all of us.

Later that evening Ike's daddy beat him bad, but Ike never told him who else was in on the deal. Ike was a tough kid. The whipping he got may have been a blessing in disguise, for one result was a ruptured eardrum that kept him out of the military. Twenty years later, standing with me at Kenny's grave, he had no idea what I meant when I likened Kenny's death to old Betsy's. Maybe I didn't either.

Jesus, we were something, Kenny and me, when we joined up back in '67. There was no calendar in those days, no sense of time, the passing days and weeks no more noticed than the leaves rattling around at night in the battalion quadrangle. We went through basic and AIT and jump school together, all the way to the 82nd at Fort Bragg, not fifty miles from where we started. Through the summer and autumn of 1967 we played war, jumping countless times from C-130s and 141s onto Bragg's sandy drop zones, laughing, daisy chaining, eager to fuck with the Hawk. In the barracks and dayrooms the talk always centered around the 'Nam, a line drawn sharply between those who had been and those who hadn't. "It don't mean nothin'," they'd say, those who had been, with the casual indifference of those who knew that it meant everything. We were all young and frisky, aching to kill someone.

Winter came and we went; the entire 3rd Brigade was sent across the pond. Me and Kenny stayed close by each other. They put us up with guys from the Americal Division to get acclimated, guys who taught us to shoot first and worry later. The first couple of nights on the perimeter we went wild, firing at every imagined sound beyond the concertina wire. One man would start, and in the blink of an eye everyone on the wire was blasting away, fiery tracers arcing across the valley in front of us, our bullets unimpeded by the apparitions moving just beyond the concertina.

After a couple of weeks with the Americal, we moved north, up near Hue, and things got serious. We started working nights and sleeping days, setting up ambushes in free-fire zones, trying to make it dangerous to walk around after dark. Mostly it was being alone all night, listening to faraway sounds telling stories. Periodic dull booms would roll across the darkened land, harassment and interdiction artillery fire. Occasionally, unseen in the darkness, the swift passage of a helicopter, someone getting over. Often, at a great distance, the crackle of small arms fire, maybe someone getting lucky, most likely a bunch of cowboys on a perimeter at some firebase. Mornings we'd pick up the Claymores, load into a slick, and fly back to camp for powdered eggs and coffee. *It don't mean nothin'.*

Time in-country was like an old bum shuffling around the corner, come and gone with no notice. The days blended seamlessly into weeks and then months, life before the 'Nam ever more shadowy and indistinct. It was like Kenny and me had been there forever, Johnston County harder and harder to relate to. Everybody in the squad changed, some a little, some a lot. One guy was killed and another got shot up real bad. Most of us figured he wouldn't make it, at least not all in one piece. Our squad leader got his third stripe and malaria on the same day. Another squadmate went off to R&R in Hawaii and we never saw him again. The lieutenant told us the word from brigade was that he got into a fight in a bar in Honolulu and killed some guy. In the end, only three of the original squad from Fort Bragg left the 'Nam together at the end of the tour: Kenny and me and a fellow named Ed Smith. One of the guys, I forget his name, got unlucky right at the end and was killed with only ten days to go.

Folks at home didn't seem to have noticed that we'd even been gone. They knew we'd been in the army and a few of them even knew we'd been overseas, but for the most part Vietnam didn't loom large in the overall scheme of things in Johnston County. Kenny moved back in with his daddy, and I rented a room from old Mrs. Herman. We had enough money saved up from the army that we didn't have to go to work right away, so we just sort of eased back into civilian life, not doing much of anything. I guess it must have been about then that Kenny started hearing voices.

"It's the boys," he told me one afternoon as we sat fishing in a pond on Bobby Euer's land. "The boys from the squad. The ones that was killed. They talk to me from time to time."

I was concentrating on my line, thinking maybe a small-mouth bass might be nibbling. "What do they say to you?" I asked.

Kenny shook his head. "Nothing much. Just that they miss us and the good times we had back at Bragg and in the 'Nam." He looked at me. "You don't think I'm crazy, do you?"

"No." I reeled in my line. The bait was gone. "But I don't believe I'd go telling a whole lot of people."

Spring ripened into summer and our dead squadmates continued to trouble Kenny. He started drinking, trying to find a place where folks would leave him alone, but to no avail. Then, in July, he borrowed his daddy's car and drove over to Durham where he was arrested for talking to himself in the parking lot of the Sears Roebuck store. When they found out he was a veteran, they transferred him over to the big VA mental hospital at Camp Butner. They kept him for the better part of a year, and every Sunday his daddy and I would drive over and visit him. If the weather was nice my landlady, Mrs. Herman, would put up some fried chicken and potato salad for us to take along or either we'd stop for barbecue and Brunswick stew—whatever we thought Kenny might enjoy.

I took a job over in Raleigh driving a delivery truck for an auto supply store and started seeing a girl who worked for the phone company. Kenny was getting a little better, and the doctors talked about letting him come home on the weekends. The first weekend he was home he told me that the dead guys from the squad still talked to him every now and again.

"I know better than to tell the doctors at Butner about it, though," he said. He leaned in close to me—he didn't want his daddy, who was out in the kitchen, hearing him. "I tell you, Billy, it's not so bad, not so bad at all."

"What's not so bad, Kenny?"

"Where they are. A lot of guys are there with them. All guys from the 'Nam. And listen." He checked to make sure his daddy was still out of earshot. "We could have gone with them. Still can. They're waiting for us. Me and you and the rest of the guys."

I shook my head. "They'll have a by-God long wait for me," I told him. "I ain't planning on dying anytime soon."

Kenny smiled and wouldn't talk about it anymore.

November came and went, and I had to move out of Mrs. Herman's place when she caught me with my friend from the phone company in my room. I bought a used Plymouth and an old house trailer that Gene Patterson let me set up on some property he owned down by the river. It didn't have any electric nor running water but I fixed up a propane heater to keep it warm, and it was all a fellow needed. In December, right before the holidays, Kenny was discharged from out at Butner and moved back in with his daddy. At first, things seemed to be going all right, but by January Kenny was drinking again, and he and his daddy were fighting all the time.

Finally his daddy threw him out, and he moved into the trailer with me. Kenny cut down on his drinking, mainly because his money was mostly gone, and I wasn't making enough to more than feed us and fill up the propane tank. I'd get home at night and we'd eat something and drink a few beers and talk about the guys. My girl from the phone company wouldn't come out to the trailer after Kenny moved in.

It was in February that Kenny killed himself. I had gone to work that morning after we came in from Gene's pond and I guess he sat around the trailer most of the day thinking about it. I mind it was a cold day, bitter cold, with a low, gray sky that seemed to come right down to the ground. Occasional bursts of rain splattered against the trailer's metal sides like buckshot. It was already dark when I got back from Raleigh with some take-out chicken and coleslaw for our dinner. Kenny was on the floor of the trailer, most of his head gone from the shotgun blast.

The county took his veteran's burial allowance and buried him in a public plot just outside Smithfield. Kenny didn't belong to no church, so I asked the preacher from a Free Will Baptist Church my momma had gone to to say the service. It was a simple affair. As the plain, aluminum VA coffin was lowered into the ground, all I could think about was me and

Kenny joining the army together. I had to turn sort of sideways at the grave because I didn't want Ike to see me crying.

After he died, I worried for the longest time that maybe Kenny or some of the other guys might start talking to me, like they did him. I laid awake to all hours of the night, listening, but I never heard a thing.

Coming Next Month—

CUTDOWN

by John A. Miller

The first full-length work of fiction from award-winning author John A. Miller, *CUTDOWN* is a stunning debut, with rich storytelling and intense narrative drive, reminiscent of the best work of Stephen Hunter and James Lee Burke. Gritty and evocative, *CUTDOWN* introduces Claude McCutcheon, one of the most memorably independent and sardonic characters ever to take center stage in suspense fiction.

Turn the page for a special preview of *CUTDOWN*, an April 1997 Pocket Books Hardcover.

Axis Prisoner-of-War Compound
Camp Lee, Virginia
August 10, 1943

In the predawn darkness the swiftly flowing Appomattox River was an undulating black ribbon, its smooth surface blending seamlessly with the steep, heavily overgrown banks on either side. Although the eastern horizon bore a faint promise of the coming day, the river and its environs lay shrouded in darkness so complete that even an alert observer would likely have missed the young man picking his way carefully down to the water. He was hot, thirsty, and very tired, but he was a soldier and moved with great discipline. When he escaped from the compound shortly after midnight he had had no idea that a river would be there but had somehow sensed, long before he came upon it, that such a body awaited him. His determination was such that upon reaching it, despite a primordial fear of what might lie beneath its stygian surface, he scarcely paused. *Better to drown,* he thought, *better to die than to remain caged with men who have surrendered.* So silently did he enter the river that it was as if some sort of reptilian predator had slid off the bank, leaving a soundless wake in the black water and a breath of fear on the shore.

To the east a wan, penumbral glow appeared on the horizon, an illumination not yet dawn but nonetheless sufficient to begin turning formless shadows into almost-distinct objects. The young soldier pulled himself ashore where a tangle of vines and bushes overhung the river, obscuring any sign of transit from water to land. He slept much of the day, waking occasionally to mentally catalog the rural sounds washing over the river and its environs: dogs barking, the occasional lowing of a cow, and once, at a distance, two boys laughing. When darkness was again complete, two full hours after the sun had set, he reentered the river and was swallowed by the night.

Southern Railroad's locomotive number 209 sat fretfully waiting just outside the roundhouse, not moving and yet not completely still. The fireman was stoking the firebox even as the engineer leaned out to search ahead for the conductor's signal to move forward. The Richmond, Virginia, marshaling yard was a maze of railroad tracks and sidings full of freight cars being herded into trains for destinations south and west. It was almost 1:00 A.M. and a heavy fog muffled the sharp noises of steel on steel. The engineer of number 209 saw his conductor's signal and eased the massive General Motors steam locomotive forward. After swinging aboard as 209 passed abreast of him, the conductor directed the engineer through the marshaling yard to the waiting train of forty-three cars. There were forty-one cars full of olive drab combat fatigues and leather boots bound for Fort Benning, in Georgia, and two empty "deadheads" belonging to the Southern Pacific Railroad Company being routed to Dallas. The fireman and his engineer lit cigarettes and gossiped quietly while the conductor picked up the final manifest documents from the dispatcher's tower.

Unseen by the train's crew, the soldier slipped across the adjoining tracks in the fog and darkness and quickly climbed into one of the deadheads, pulling the large door shut behind him. He leaned against one wall of the car and slid slowly down onto his haunches, exhaustion seeping over him like water. He had no idea where the train might be going but knew that each mile, in whatever direction, between him and the place from which he had escaped was a mile closer to home. Home. *Is it truly possible? From such a distance?*

The screech of wood against metal as the boxcar's door was suddenly pulled open startled him out of his reverie. He cursed himself for his carelessness, for giving in to fatigue and hunger before the train was actually under way. He rose to a crouch, a knife held low in his right hand, his dilated eyes searching for danger.

A railroad detective pulled himself up into the darkened car with a curse, a flashlight in one hand and a wicked-looking piece of angle iron held menacingly overhead with the other. He was a big man, with an air of casual brutality about him.

"All right," he growled, playing the flashlight beam toward the opposite end of the car, "whoever the hell's in here damn well better . . ."

Without thought the young soldier stepped up silently

from behind and threw a rock-hard forearm around the yard bull's neck, pulling him backward while simultaneously driving the five-inch knife blade into his lower back and right kidney. The pain, so intense and sudden, paralyzed the man in the soldier's unrelenting grasp. The soldier withdrew the knife, then instantly plunged it again into the yard bull's back, piercing the left ventricle of his heart.

Death came so unexpectedly that the yard bull experienced no fear. The pain of the first wound precluded struggle or thought, and the terrible swiftness of the second ended his life before he knew he was in danger.

The soldier carefully lowered the body to the floor, then quickly re-closed the boxcar's door and stood listening intently for voices or footsteps, keenly and unhappily aware that his hoped-for conveyance to freedom was also a trap with only one exit. Only when the train's departure was announced with a jolt did his heartbeat begin to slow and his muscles relax. *Westward,* he thought, as if by force of will alone he could point the locomotive in the direction he wanted it to go.

Half a world away from the forests of his youth and only vaguely aware of the actual geography and landscape, of the political and economic boundaries and borders between where he was and where he needed to be, the soldier nonetheless urged the train *westward* as slowly it began to move. Inside the boxcar he felt only a disembodied sense of movement as the train gradually picked up speed. And later, splitting the night, the dopplered ringing bells of road-crossing barricades approached, met, and left behind by the rushing train were the saddest sounds he thought he had ever heard.

Berkeley, California
Monday, March 7, 1994

The police sergeant at the front desk wore a simple gold earring in his right earlobe and the look of a man with little patience for human frailty. Claude McCutcheon stood in front of him for at least thirty seconds before he bothered to look up.

"Yeah?"

"I'd like to see Robert Norton," Claude said with exaggerated politeness. Casually dressed in a linen shirt and well-worn blue jeans, he could have been anywhere between thirty-five and fifty, depending on one's point of view. Too-long, sandy blond hair and a trim, hard waist made judging his age and station in life more difficult. "I understand he's being questioned with regards to a homicide."

"Who are you?"

"I'm his father," Claude responded sarcastically.

The sergeant ignored Claude and picked up the telephone. He punched in three numbers and waited until someone answered. "Norton's mouthpiece is here," he said. He listened a second, then hung up the receiver. "Room 148," he said, looking back down at his paperwork, refusing to meet Claude's eyes. He gestured over his shoulder with his right thumb. "Down the hall."

"Nice earring," Claude sneered as he walked past the desk. He walked into room 148 without bothering to knock, hoping it would offend someone. The small room was shared by four detectives, their civil-service gray-metal desks sitting cheek-by-jowl. Bobby Norton, a slender African American in his mid-forties, sat next to one of the desks. A slightly older man, also black, wearing blue jeans and a lumberjack shirt, sat behind the desk. A detective's badge was clipped to the front of his shirt. He looked at Claude and smiled. "Claude McCutcheon. I didn't know you'd started chasing criminal work."

Claude shook hands with the detective. The two men had known each other, though not well, for a number of years. Jim Malone was a big man, as tall as Claude, and heavy-set, with burly shoulders and a gut gone to seed. He had spent twenty years as a military policeman, retiring in 1985 with the rank of major. He joined the Berkeley Police Department in 1986 as head of the criminal investigation division.

"I haven't," Claude said, nodding at Bobby. "I'm here strictly as a favor to Mr. Norton. In any event, based on what he told my secretary over the telephone, I'm not sure he even needs an attorney. Am I correct in assuming that he is not a suspect in the homicide in question?"

"That's correct," Jim Malone said. "He was at the scene, though, and so naturally we're interested in any information he might be able to provide us."

"Do you mind if I speak with Mr. Norton in private for a few minutes?"

"No problem," Malone said. "Use room 152, two doors down. It's an interrogation room. I'll see that no one bothers you."

"Come on." Claude took Bobby's arm and maneuvered him out of the detectives' office.

"Aren't we going in there?" Bobby asked as the two of them passed room 152 and continued down the hall.

"You should know better than that," Claude said as

they exited the police station proper and stood on the back steps. "There's more microphones hidden in there than in the American embassy in Moscow. We'll talk out here."

"Man, am I glad to see you," Bobby said as he took one of Claude's cigarettes. He was rather nattily dressed in linen trousers, a silk Italian shirt, and faux-crocodile slip-ons.

"Why? If you were just a witness, what the fuck did you need me to hot-foot it down here for?"

Bobby shook his head. "Listen," he said, his tone of voice implying wonder that anyone would ask such a question, particularly someone who knew that there's no such thing as a confidential conversation anywhere in a police station. "There ain't no way I'm talking to the police in no murder situation without my attorney present."

"I'm not your attorney." Claude lowered his eyebrows and looked hard at Bobby. "What the fuck's going on here? Who exactly was killed?"

Bobby smiled and briskly rubbed his hands together. "That's what I'm trying to tell you. It was Myron Hirsch who was killed."

"Myron Hirsch? The lawyer?"

"That's the one," Bobby said. "Do you know him?"

Claude shook his head. "I know enough to know that everyone thought he was an asshole. He's a loose cannon on the lunatic fringe of the environmental movement. Or was. He got a lot of press a year or two ago by advocating the lynching of Interior Department officials for authorizing timber harvesting on federal land." He paused for a second, remembering the business at hand. "Where the hell were you when Hirsch got done?"

"Upstairs. See, I had gone over to the boat to see Hirsch about some business."

"What boat? And what sort of business?"

"He lived on a houseboat out at the Berkeley marina. And the business was about my place in Richmond." Bobby ran a small after-hours nightclub in Richmond, California, across the bay from San Francisco. "He was wanting to raise my rent, and we been arguing over some repairs he was supposed to do."

"You mean Hirsch owned the building your club is in?"

"Yeah. Anyway, I went over to his boat to try and settle things with him." Bobby paused and ground out his cigarette on the pavement. "I could see when I got there that he was nervous about something, wanted me to leave, you know? Anyway, I told him I wasn't leaving until we got some sort of understanding on my rent and the repairs. Right then he heard someone coming down the pier to his boat and he told me to wait upstairs. Said his business with this other person wouldn't take long. I would have left but I could see something big was going on and figured maybe if I stayed around I might pick up on something. To help me out, you know what I'm saying? So I go upstairs and, man, no sooner do I get there than the shooting starts. I mean, they don't say more than a couple of words to each other and then it's over." Bobby shook his head at the wonder of it all. "Shot the motherfucker right in the heart."

"Did you see the killer?"

Bobby laughed, a high-pitched, nervous laugh. "No fucking way. I didn't make a sound. I figured if the killer knew I was upstairs he'd done me too."

Claude smiled. "Were you scared?"

"Shit." All the mirth left Bobby's face. "Wouldn't you have been? I didn't have no piece or nothing on me. I stayed up there and tried not to breathe too loud."

"Could you make out what the killer and Hirsch said to each other before the shooting?"

Bobby shook his head. "No, I couldn't. I never heard the killer at all, just Hirsch laughing and saying something like 'Sue me.'"

"So what happened next?"

"I heard the killer rootin' around Hirsch's office looking for something, tearing drawers open, throwing papers around, shit like that. Then someone else comes down the pier and onto the boat. Police say it was the harbormaster. Anyway, he comes onto the boat and into Hirsch's office and gets himself whacked on the head. Then the killer leaves."

"What did you do then?"

"I waited a while to make sure he had really left, you know? Then, when I hear the harbormaster groaning downstairs, I figure it's time to call the police."

"That's all? You called the police and that was the end of it? How was the harbormaster?"

"Man, he was bleeding bad," Bobby said. "I almost tried to help him but then I thought about all that AIDS shit with blood and all, so I just waited out in the parking lot until the police came. The medics said he would be okay."

Claude shook his head. "That's the goddamnedest story I ever heard. Did you tell all this to the detectives inside?" He nodded toward the police building.

"I told them everything I just told you."

"Well, let's go back inside and see if we can wrap this up."

The two men reentered the building and walked down

the hall to room 148. As soon as they walked into the room one of the younger detectives angrily accosted them.

"Why didn't you use room 152 like Detective Malone told you?" he asked.

Claude looked at him for a long second as one might look at a particularly annoying child and then turned to Malone. "Have you finished questioning Mr. Norton for the time being?" he asked, pointedly ignoring the younger detective's question.

Malone smiled and waved his colleague back to his desk. "Yeah, Claude, I guess we have everything we need for now. We know where to reach him if we think of anything else."

Outside the police station Claude and Bobby shook hands next to Claude's truck, a decidedly unrestored 1955 Chevrolet pickup Claude had owned for some eight years.

"Man, I appreciate you coming down like this." Bobby looked at the truck and shook his head, clearly appalled that his friend would drive such a low-rent vehicle.

Claude shrugged. "I'd say that it was hardly necessary, especially since you'd already told them everything you knew." He looked closely at Bobby. "You did tell them everything, didn't you? You're not holding anything back?"

"No way, man. What I know, they know." He looked again at the truck, seemingly unable to take his eyes off it. "I don't know how you expect to attract the right kind of clients driving this thing around."

"I wouldn't be standing too close to it in those nice clothes," Claude advised dryly. "You get some of that oxidized paint on those slacks, and even Sal's Army won't take them." He opened the door and got up into the cab. "Listen," he said, leaning out the driver's side window, "call me if anything else comes up. No, wait a minute. Don't call me." Claude jerked a thumb back in the direction of the police station. "Call Malone." He smiled to take some of the edge off his words. "And be careful until Malone bags someone."

New London, California
Tuesday, March 8, 1994

Margaret Stewart Tikkanen, like her father and grandfather before her, considered the greater part of Humboldt County, in northern California, to be hers in the way others consider their automobiles, or their dogs, or their power tools to be their personal property. She and her father, Joseph Tikkanen, owned not only the Northwestern Lumber Company and all of its lands in fee simple, but also the Eel River Railroad Company and all of its right-of-way from Eureka, California, south to San Francisco and north to Portland. She sometimes considered the men and women who worked for her to be little more than another form of chattel property, assets not unlike the company-owned houses they occupied in New London, one of California's last company towns. Margaret's father, Joseph, had inherited everything—the company, the railroad, the vast real estate holdings, and the employees—from his father-in-law, her grandfather, F. M. Stewart, a man who believed in the divine sanctity of mercantile power. "Mr. Norton has disappeared," Margaret informed her father as she walked into his office. She handed him a copy of the *Oakland Tribune*, which featured the headline "Radical Environmentalist Murdered." A tall woman, with shoulder-length hair more red than auburn, she would have been considered extremely attractive by any objective standard had her sharply chiseled face had even a hint of softness about it. As it was, she was frankly admired whenever she entered a public room, particularly by those who did not know her. Her eyes were an astonishing blue and her body was hard and fit, both physical attributes directly linked to the Finnish gene pool from which her father had emerged. Margaret had chosen Stanford for her undergraduate education, matriculating there in the fall of 1968. She graduated in 1972 with an honors degree in economics and, at Joseph's urging, spent the following two years obtaining an MBA at Harvard. While at Cambridge she took her first lover, an energetic young instructor of Constitutional law at Harvard Law School with a taste for radical politics and fast cars. She let him drive her Porsche and used him as one might use a particularly comfortable pair of shoes—rather too often than is good for the long term. At the end of her second and final year she sold the Porsche and had his belongings removed without warning from her luxurious town home on the James River.

Joseph Tikkannen looked up from the papers on his desk. Although Margaret had taken over the day-to-day operation of the company, she still looked to Joseph for advice and consent on strategic issues and major capital expenditures. Father and daughter shared, in addition to an uncanny physical resemblance that transcended x and y chromosomes, an unconscious bearing of authority that more often than not bordered on threat. "What does that mean?"

Margaret shook her head. "Impossible to say. Someone may have gotten to him. Or, he could be getting ready to offer something for sale to the highest bidder."

Joseph grunted. "What about his lawyer, this McCutcheon."

"He claims not to represent Norton although our contact in the Berkeley Police Department says that the detective heading up the investigation isn't so sure. But even if he's not actually representing Norton, my guess is that he's either gotten or he's trying to get his finger into the pie."

"You think McCutcheon's involved?"

"I think he is now. We know from our contact that Hirsch wasn't expecting Norton to show up when he did." Margaret smiled, a nonhumorous facial expression feared by all who worked at the Northwestern Lumber Company. "When a two-bit crook needs help selling stolen goods, who better to call than a lawyer?"

"I take it then that you wish to ignore the missing Mr. Norton for the time being and concentrate on lawyer McCutcheon."

"That is precisely what I intend to do."

Joseph sat back in his chair. "You might consider calling one of our 'friends' in Sacramento for some assistance. It could be that McCutcheon, like many lawyers, has political aspirations."

Margaret nodded. She knew that from the moment he had taken control of the company upon the death of her grandfather in 1952, her father had recognized that the post-war era would be characterized by an increasingly adversarial relationship between business and government, an extraordinarily prescient view given that he had emigrated to the United States from Finland only

four years earlier. During the almost unbelievably prof-
itable decades of the 1950s and 1960s, when most
businessmen were unable to see beyond their ever-
fattening bottom lines, Joseph was slowly and deliberately developing a political power base not only in
Humboldt County but also in Sacramento and Washington, D.C. He taught her that money, and money alone,
was the key that unlocked the door to legislative
access—it was, as one former Speaker of the House so
eloquently put it, the mother's milk of electoral politics.
Numerous political careers at the local, state, and federal level were started and maintained with money
provided by the Northwestern Lumber Company, most
of it in the form of cash and none of it directly traceable
back to the company. Joseph's success as a patron of the
democratic process was staggering. Over the years Joseph, and later Margaret, counted among their posses-
sions four members of the Congress of the United States
(three representatives and one senator), seven assem-
blymen in Sacramento, including three successive
speakers of California's House, and every governor,
Democratic and Republican, elected since 1958. The
company demanded relatively little for its money, re-
quiring only that the men (and later women) it bought
be unwavering (not to mention successful) in their
efforts to turn aside, by whatever means necessary, all
attempts to regulate the lumber business or to insert the
governmental bureaucracy into the intimate and deli-
cate relationship existing between employer and em-
ployee.

The first priority, Joseph repeatedly impressed on
Margaret when he first revealed to her the nature and
extent of the company's illegal political payments, must
always be absolute security regarding the knowledge of

these matters. He showed her how he recorded every name, every payment, every vote purchased on specific legislation of particular interest and importance to the company in a journal he kept under tight lock and key in his office safe.

Margaret eagerly supported, and in a number of significant ways expanded upon, her father's vision when she took over active management of the company. Locally, she went far beyond the mere clandestine distribution of cash to elected officials and political aspirants. She publicly provided the funds needed for a new county medical center in Eureka, established a scholarship fund for the sons and daughters of all county employees, and fully endowed the School of Forestry at Humboldt State College. She became the patron saint of all the county's law enforcement and fire control agencies with the establishment of a trust fund to care for the families of any officer who might die in the line of duty. In all, her careful financial largese created an atmosphere throughout the county wherein one publicly criticized the Northwestern Lumber Company at one's own substantial personal risk.

"I'll keep that in mind," she said. "Right now I want to develop as much background information as I can on McCutcheon. We have to know what sort of leverage we can use against him when the need arises."

Don't miss
CUTDOWN
An April 1997 Pocket Books Hardcover